we don't listen to them

Also by Sean Johnston:

A Day Does Not Go By
Bull Island
A Long Day Inside the Buildings (with Drew Kennickell)
All This Town Remembers
The Ditch Was Lit Like This
Listen All You Bullets

we don't listen to them

Sean Johnston

thistledown press

Library and Archives Canada Cataloguing in Publication
Johnston, Sean, 1966-, author
We don't listen to them / Sean Johnston.
Issued in print and electronic formats.
ISBN 978-1-927068-92-2 (pbk.).– ISBN 978-1-77187-008-5 (html).–
ISBN 978-1-77187-009-2 (pdf)

I. Title.
PS8569.O391738W42 2014 C813'.6 C2014-905351-7
C2014-905352-5

Cover and book design by Jackie Forrie
Printed and bound in Canada

Thistledown Press Ltd.
410 2nd Avenue North
Saskatoon, Saskatchewan, S7K 2C3
www.thistledownpress.com

Canadian Heritage Patrimoine canadien

Canada Council for the Arts Conseil des Arts du Canada

Thistledown Press gratefully acknowledges the financial assistance of the Canada Council for the Arts, the Saskatchewan Arts Board, and the Government of Canada through the Canada Book Fund for its publishing program.

for Finley and Lucy

Contents

How Blue

THIS MAD FUCKER ROLLED BY HIM real fast, which was stupid, because he was carrying an ice cream cone and he almost dropped it. His mother would have been pissed. He would have dropped it right on his shirt. Why would that be his fault anyways?

Stupid. Ronny licked the purple ice cream quickly, in case there were other skateboarders on the way. In fact, never mind. He sat down on the curb to eat it. Who cares?

His father was walking up the street. Oh no. He was late. Oh no, his father would see him. What kind of a man wears a dark suit like that here in the suburbs on a sunny day. Question? No. A statement. But you don't need a black suit, that's for sure. An ice cream cone is what you need. Purple. That big book his dad reads while he chuckles madly to himself. Never mind. Get ready.

"Hi Dad."

"Hi chum."

Who is that coming out of the door? Oh Christ, it's that dumb old lady from church. His dad will stand and talk to her, though Ronny hears every Sunday evening that she is a hypocrite. He hears it through the walls, along with stuff like take that hat off. It's inappropriate. And so on. Why?

There was a lot he wanted explained.

"Hello Mr. Wilson," the old hypocrite said.

"Good afternoon, Minnie," his father said. "I am just walking home by my son on the sidewalk. He's enjoying this purple cone while sitting on the curb."

"Of course," she said. "Now listen. We have to get a few things straight here."

"Absolutely, straight is the best way, I am sure," he said.

Ronny licked the ice cream and watched his dad's moustache. He needed moustache wax or something. Ronny saw old guys in cartoons with sharp-ended moustaches big as some kind of wild animal's horns. Instead, his dad wore a new-fashioned moustache that was shaped like a broom. Sometimes when he laughed it looked like his teeth hung directly from the moustache. Now that is cartoony in a bad way.

It appears he has no lips at all. Ronny shook his head sadly and imprinted his own cold lips on the purple cone. Who invented purple? Some people would call it pink but he knows it's purple. Some people think wrong.

His dad was going on and on. They would both be late. But at least on the car ride over for pizza, his father would tell stories about the sorry old bitch he was jabbering to now.

"Listen, Ronny. Do you hear what Ms. Smith is saying?"

The old woman shaking her head, tsking, tsking.

"It's not really the sort of thing you tell a boy, Mr. Wilson."

The big toothy smile opened up under the moustache and his dad said, "Oh, that's my mistake then. He's right here after all, a part of this very environment. If I were to describe him I would say he fits in quite nicely. A boy with an ice cream cone sitting on the curb while his elegantly dressed father speaks to one of the elderly ladies from church."

The old lady with her old dress and her big dumb nose just stared at his father. Ha.

"Yet I suppose you're right. An intervention is not best subject for a boy. Drugs, right?"

"Booze," she said.

There is a lot of stuff that is bad but booze is the worst. Sometimes the kids that make him smoke are drunk. Sometimes they must be. You see it on TV. Sometimes he hears about the booze through walls. Wait a minute.

He stood up off the curb and stepped close to his father. With his coneless hand he reached for his father's free hand. Wait a minute. A quick lick of the ice cream before his father leaned down. If he did. He did.

He leans down to kiss him on the top of the head when he's been drinking. That's the booze all right. He can smell it. Step a little closer you old hag. Why can't a man enjoy a drink with his friends, and so on. The bottle, his old aunt called it. But she lived in a different province or state. Here they call it booze.

He kept missing pieces of the conversation. But this is good ice cream. Glad to get the waffle cone too. Old cones are stupid; they only get their flavour from the ice cream. This is from the cone itself. Waffle. Not really waffle but still. Waffle.

"Hey buddy, this nice church lady is coming over to our house tonight."

"What?" said the boy.

"Mizz Smith," his dad said. "Mizz Smith is coming to our house."

Both those characters stared at each other not saying anything. Can the booze just hit a man like that all of a sudden? The old woman wasn't wearing anything on her feet. That's odd. But, odder still is the look on her face. That's right. He had two more bites left on his cone. That's right, my dad is on the booze. He's tied one on after work, I guess. Now Mom will have to drive —

"Aren't we going out to the Mediterranean Inn tonight?"

"Oh no," his father said, rubbing the top of the boy's head. "Oh no. Your mother has invited this fine woman over for the evening. We mustn't be going to that local pizza place tonight after all."

The teeth under the moustache get bigger and bigger. But that's right, Mizz something — Smith — you keep screwing your mouth up like that. No lips on her, either, just a colourless hole like the one under the cat's tail. The cat at her feet. Get the cat back in the house, Mizz.

She didn't notice anything. She leaned ahead and hissed in his father's ear.

"Oh fuck. Just for your years of service then, sure," he said and hugged her in his arms. The purple cone was all gone and the old lady's face was blank and white.

Oh Jesus, the booze. It was all right. It's the booze never mind. No problem.

"I am so tired," his father said, and took his jacket off. "It's the sun."

Well, it is inappropriate to wear all that black in the sun. It's not right. Not walking home like that. Where's the car? How could they go to the pizza place anyway? Where's the car? That mad fucker made him sit down on the curb with his ice cream because you don't want that purple on your shirt when you're going out to dinner. Your mother might not be as nice as your dad.

"Let's have the intervention right here," his dad said.

Not here. Where is here? Only two blocks from their house. Let's go home.

"Yup. That's a great idea," his father said. He kicked his shoes off and stepped onto the lawn in his socks. Then he sat down and took his socks off. He didn't want to get back up. Ronny sat beside him and the nosey old bitch's cat came to lick his fingers.

"I don't want to stand up," his father said, leaning back to stretch fully out. He stared at the sky. Ronny did too, but the old woman was on her phone. Soon his dad was snoring and Ronny was lying on the ground looking up at the clouds. There were only two and you can't say they were any shape at all. One of them wanted to be a square and one of them wanted to be a circle; neither of them wanted to be a duck or a horse.

Mizz whatever, did she? She must have thought his eyes were closed. She must have thought she was wearing something under her skirt, who knows? The older boys who make Ronny smoke talk about things but this can't be the thing they talk about. Why did she have to walk over him? Never mind. She was in her house.

This nervous guy who plays with his watch at the back of the church drove up in a wine-coloured Lincoln. He honked the horn and his father woke up. When he saw the car he smiled and had a burst of energy.

"You want to sit in the front, Ronny?"

Not really no he didn't. It's hot and the seats are always heated. Why can't you turn the seats off? Why can't you turn the heat off? His father started snoring in the back seat.

"Let's go get some pizza you mad fucker!" Ronny yelled. "Let's get my mom."

The man said don't say fucker and also Ronny's mom didn't want pizza. But we're all going to get some coffee and some pizza, sure. Why not?

Was it the last straw? Ronny asked the man. Was his sorry ass out of here? Was it high time he stopped fucking up?

The man stared straight ahead and handed Ronny a piece of gum. It was mint. Who wants minty gum? Grown-ups like old-fashioned flavours, not stuff that makes your tongue purple.

But doesn't he love her? Isn't it going to get better? Ronny wanted to ask. What about the things he can't hear? What about the way they come out in the morning with red eyes and embarrassed smiles, making pancakes for him even though he already had toast? What about the cartoons he watches while they smile for some reason across him?

His father and mother always agree those hypocrites don't know a thing about love. What about all the windows being open in the morning and the air being fresh as hell while his father stands bare-chested in the kitchen, smiling?

We Don't Celebrate That

WE HAVE JUST RECEIVED THE NEW rules, and, of course, they are not that different from the old ones. Now we sit at our machines typing in accordance with the new rules, thinking we fully understand them. I hear someone in the next cube laughing to himself, but is it his keyboard I hear, or a neighbouring keyboard? How can he be laughing if he's understood the new rules?

As I say, most of them are the same — variations on the theme of do not make the prime minister into a caricature. We all know that by now, and how can you laugh knowing there is someone deciding if a human is a cartoon? In fact, my neighbour, the cackling hero, Paul Binchy, cannot help but recall the odd case of an old, a mutual, friend who became famous. His pseudonym was Jim Zero. He wrote the right stories his whole life, and, as a matter of fact, he was very good.

These stories inhabited this very world, they grew out of our own concerns but they were about love, for instance, or the way a man may honour his own memory in his small village. His popularity became too great, and the prime minister read his books, commented on them in public, and even dined with Jim Zero at times. Pretend I don't know that. Jim Zero was never seen in public. It could have been anybody, but I had to disappear at the same time.

Jim Zero did well until someone from the university published a paper in a journal way over in New Zealand explaining how these subtleties must be read. The prime minister is absent, he wrote, not because there was nothing to ridicule, but because the rollicking comedy of the novels could not exist in a world which also contained the prime minister. Jim Zero is gone, to be sure, though it's impossible to know which one of our colleagues used that name. The name is gone.

We are here because we are good at what we do, but the keyboard doesn't measure your laughter. Paul has no need to laugh. None of us believe him. None of us think this is funny.

The new section of the rules, section 18, for example. There is only one rule in this section: All stories must say what they are not.

Paul on the bus this morning was all smiles. It's the first day of the new paradigm, he told me, as he sat down.

Yeah, I said. That's great.

It is, he said.

Irony is closely monitored, I told him quietly, leaning toward him.

It's not irony, he told me, and kept up with the smiling. Besides, nobody watches everything. They'd need as many people watching as being watched. That's insane. Let's not be paranoid.

Yeah, I told him. You're right. But a man makes a joke now and then.

Cripes, you're depressing.

Maybe it's the rules.

Fuck the rules, JP. They're no different. They're the same. Actually, we should celebrate how little has changed. That's the glass half full, right? This is the same day as it was before the new paradigm.

Even calling it that —

You're right. Let's talk about something else.

I stared at my hands, which were folded on my lap, while the polite whirring of the bus lulled me. I am always comforted by machines running as they should. I resisted that, in the old days — of course, I never wrote about it, due to the symbolic repercussions. My colleagues would have ridiculed me. Even under a pseudonym, I avoided describing any character being soothed by the old well-oiled machine, all its parts working in concert, accepting their roles in the larger metal and electric scheme.

As I've aged, I appreciate more the body's mechanical aspects; the body is also a machine, though we lack a complete comprehension of it. It is something, this spark of life, etc.

I've been without use of my limbs. I have lived in a weakened body where my intellect limped along the physical edges, wondering at its own mobility, trying to find energy somewhere in its dying machine —

I was distracted by Paul looking over me and out the window. We were stopped in the protest block. We began moving again. I saw signs, bright signs with big black letters: NO WATER DEAL! YANKEES DON'T MAKE THE RULES! and so on. We stopped one more time on the protest block, to let someone off. I watched him put on his approved vest and stand beside another man. This man had no vest. His sign was full of smaller letters: We know what the Americans are doing / they're not coming up behind us they've come / right up FRONT: they see this as some kind of virtue —

As the bus began moving again, we each resumed our straight-ahead gaze.

Lesley has been accepted at the university, Paul said.

Fantastic, I told him. What in?

Engineering, he said, and I understood his mood. There is no ideology in building a bridge. Nobody will ask you to spell out in concrete what is and is not contained in the concrete. This is not a jungle gym, you won't say. This is not a glass box for trinkets. This is not a church, either legal or discouraged. This is not for airplanes. Everyone knows what a bridge is.

~

I'm having the time of my life, Paul tells me. I've been working for weeks and produced nothing new. I'm going to make this my life's work. I don't care what it takes. I don't have a system. I think I need an assistant.

That's a sure sign, I tell him. I think you're destined for management.

He's smiling, but he stops. No management, he says. Listen, you know me. I am about to become horribly grand, but it will just be for a moment; you know I think it's all horseshit.

Yeah, I tell him.

I think this is my best work, he whispers.

I know what he means. He means he thinks he is producing art. I'm moved to give him a small hug, which we don't do. But today we do. We never use the word anymore, but we know when we say it.

I wanted to support him. I did. I pictured him listing things, describing them, happy as he'd ever been. He could work on a project that would never end, a book that contained everything, but said it did not.

Part of me got angry. Angry at Joyce, who was so far up the academy as to be harmless and comical. Who needs another subversive story?

But my own experience, which, to be honest, frightened me, and the thought of Paul happy, working on his masterwork, saved by the fact it would never be read — why not? He's worked hard his whole life.

~

He writes:

This is not a story about the time Paul Binchy was walking from a small restaurant in his youth. Not about the small delay in his life when he met a friend of his father's on the relatively quiet October street. On that day there was no sun above and its light didn't end on the dirty cold asphalt. It's not about the cold from the shade that made him shiver as his father's friend spoke.

It's about —

Paul, I said, we don't have to say what it's about, exactly, if I understand the new rules —

No. You're right, he says. We don't.

But you're telling what it's about.

So? Listen. It's about.

It's about. Don't say what it's about. We still have the illusion, I tell him. The vivid continuous dream and so on.

What?

The suspension of—

No. It's all bullshit now. All bets are off.

But you're actually, I tell him, through this list . . .

Paul isn't listening anymore. He's hurt. Or angry. Angry or hurt; even in the new paradigm, a writer's ego is fragile. I should have known. We used to laugh together, working away in the word mines, thinking of new ways to say the obvious, laughing at all the things our peers were doing. Really? From the cat's point of view? Things like that.

Come on, Paul, I say. Carry on.

No. Never mind.

Well give it to me then. I'll read it.

And I do:

It's about the young man shivering there at the edge of the darkness because of a completely different reason. As the older man spoke about how mild the winter would be, digging his hands into the small pockets of his jacket, a bus pulled up beside them. As if he'd been running beside it the whole time, a man stopped suddenly as the door hissed opened. No one exited. The man stood before the open door, briefly, holding onto the small child riding on his shoulders. She reached down, removed the man's black glasses and leaned toward his naked eyes, saying, Daddy, I have to poop. They got on the bus, and it drove away.

The young man was smiling, ignoring the words of his father's friend, his mind on the man stooping carefully through the door of the bus while his daughter worked at getting his glasses back onto his face. He stared at the space the departed bus left on the street. Just where the shade met the sunned-upon asphalt, a mouse lay, almost invisible at the dark border.

The old man continued with his story, but the young man wanted to help the mouse, which was dying. He looked in the storyteller's eyes and tried to find a break in the string of words. He tried to find in those eyes, and in the rhythm of the voice, a need for some kind of rest. He waited, but the old man's back was to the mouse, whose black marble eyes, the size of its own little fists, if its hands would curl into fists, were round and open. They were glossy bubbles that showed nothing, but the tiny stomach heaved quickly, and the jaw hung open.

~

And this, reading this story, recalls a memory from my own youth, a memory in which I was absorbed in a novel. A man stood at a podium in this book. He stood and spoke to a crowd of strangers and began to lose the ability to breathe. He spoke as well as he could because the breath was leaving him. He clutched the sides of the podium. He concentrated and he was scared, but not scared enough to stop speaking.

As the description of the man's heroism or stupidity worked its way down the left page of the open book on my lap I became more and more agitated, because the book went on for at least one hundred more pages. How could this character die? Then, in my peripheral vision I saw the white space with five asterisks halfway down the page on the right.

I read as quickly as I could, knowing that if we got to the white space with the man still alive, he would survive. I was no longer angry at the man for wasting his last breaths on words. They weren't his last breaths; the white space was right there.

~

Paul and I used to sit in the Royal Oak and have dreams. We were in the journalism program with all the others, but we wanted to write stories, and we talked all the time about art. We were going to write the truth, etc. We were young.

We were with a group that went down to the United States one spring, for briefings, for press conferences, and so on, as part of the State Department's Voluntary Visitor's Program. We listened to the speeches, the evasions. We read stories the next day. We spent our per diem on beer and cheap cigarettes. Uh huh, we thought, this is why we need art. The only way at the truth anymore, and so on. We talked about some lofty things that we were still young enough to believe. We would use our middle names, for instance, as pennames. We were the first generation of prairie kids to be named after the dead or dying towns of our parents' youth — he was Paul Glamis. I was James Perdue.

~

The coincidences are awful. I came back to Ottawa from my exile just in time to get on a flight and fly out west to see my mother. They'd kept me away for almost a year, then they let me return. By then everyone had forgotten the subversive, made-up, author. I thought they were being human. But the whole thing made a good cover.

Where are your brothers? my mother asked me.

Soon, I said. We all have so much work.

I think your brothers are gone, she said, though she was blind by then. I could have been any one of her sons. I held her hand and told her, no, I've spoken with them recently.

Oh, she said, it's okay. Thank you for the love of your children, she whispered. I knew she meant my nieces and nephews. I had no idea where my own children had gone.

~

Nobody will know I did this. They might think someone else did it. But I have returned.

If it wasn't winter I couldn't handle it. If it was summer and I had to be out in the sunshine with bare arms, or have the sunshine curling into me past the edges of curtains, I couldn't bear it. I would need help. It turns every room into a white hospital room.

But it is winter, and staying indoors is not unusual. Darkness is not unusual. Skating on the canal is not unusual either, but there's no need to bare any part of your body, and even your face is hidden by a tingle pronounced in the extra pink of your cheeks. My cheeks. And if you see someone you know while you wait in line for a beaver tail, you can hide behind some kind of tissue, wiping your nose, when the spirit moves you, when the person you know is surprised to find you and reaches out a hand to touch your sleeve and say I haven't seen you forever.

I was back home, you say, and when pressed say that your mother was sick, which is not a lie.

Then you're back in your apartment and see yourself in the mirror, suddenly bunchy at the edges, suddenly spotted with uneven hairs and dry discolourations, suddenly old. How did your body rearrange itself? You can't even feel the tips of your fingers, but you feel the swollen knuckles. Do the people you meet out in the world know all of this?

~

I'm thinking of a time when there will be a final rule. I hope I may be dead by then. If that rule were in place right now, I would be compelled to tell you what this story is about. We will have come full circle — all the rules will have cancelled out. It is about a man doing his duty, I might say. A man struggling with skills he has barely learned and adapting to new rules, not for the sake of his family, which has left him. No, he is alone. It cannot be for the sake of anyone but himself. He fulfills his obligations and he enjoys it, because society benefits. Each step is a celebration of freedom and he's glad.

But those are not the rules today. Today there are different rules and I am not compelled to tell you anything, other than this is not a story about looking into your dying mother's eyes and contemplating the confusion there. It's not about peace either.

He Hasn't Been to the Bank in Weeks

When Helen was dying, I am afraid, I couldn't relate to the world just there, just right there. I couldn't see through the window of her room without trying. I thought first of a scene in a horrible movie I'd acted in as a young man. It was in a post-everything world and I knew it was bad when I'd made it.

~

He had smashed most of the glass in the building already.

He walked quietly toward the remaining half wall that looked out into the reception area. The band had been loud. Where was it now? The sledge hammer swung loosely at his side. He knocked it into a clay pot holding a large palm-like plant and watched the pot crack.

He held the handle in both hands and swung hard, breaking the pot and sending bits of organic material shaking to the carpet. He breathed deeply and listened to the silence. The earth in the pot clung to the plant's roots and he thought he loved that smell. Silence and the smell of the earth. The glass wall that awaited him was as smooth as a lake, and he saw his reflection there.

Blood was smeared on his shirt in wet paw prints. He looked at his paws and they were cut. They bled.

~

The sun shone on the gluey parking lot, and I had some minutes to watch its pretty standard illumination from her third-floor room before the nurse came in and saw me turn, dry-eyed, back toward Helen.

"I was afraid," I said, but those were not the words I meant to say.

She nodded and pressed the call button.

"She was a mammal," I told her.

"But a human in his normal erect state cannot thrive," the nurse said and she touched my living body on its shoulder.

"I will, you see, because of the father."

"Your fate can be a great big help. You're Norse, but this is mechanical."

As if the regression in her language could be a clue, I checked around. I spied a jar of leeches on the cart. Too late; they were dead.

"You should have punched air holes," I said, and she said she didn't know what I meant.

I took a big gulp and looked back to the parking lot. My car had a ring of melting snow piled around it. The night comes so early in the winter, and snow and the asphalt and the bare trees and the blue bollards with electrical outlets and the glass in the attendant's booth, they were all turning blue and I knew I couldn't but I felt like I could extend my own blue-shirted arm out the clean glass of the window and smudge the blue ring of snow out, and rescue my car without breaking anything — not the glass or the tiny car three stories below or even my thin, blue-veined arm or my delicate, effeminate, elegant fingers.

I took out my pen and clicked it, but the nurse got to the clipboard first.

"It's okay," I said. "I don't know what to put. I haven't been to the bank in weeks."

And I was hungry, suddenly. I tried to enjoy the feeling, I wanted to get lean, lie down and do sit ups, look at the nurse and raise my arms like I'd just won a race and was, of course, younger. We were all younger.

~

I kneaded Helen's shoulders and held her arms and rubbed them. I held her face in my hands and wanted to kiss those funny-coloured lips. I couldn't see the fine hair on her upper lip and was afraid they'd shaved her.

I was shocked at the ridiculous nature of my desire. I held my dead wife's best panties in my hands and slid them up her legs. They were lace. I pulled them up and snugged them tight against her.

I meant to say sorry.

It was the opposite of taking them off and I meant to say sorry. The wild unpatterned curls of pubic hair curled out of the elastic leg holes and the grey ones stuck straight out.

The body. The body, she was a mammal, as I had stupidly told my daughter on the phone after making the same mistake with the nurse and I was so glad I was dressing Helen alone.

I was as hard as when I was a boy and I felt my face burn with shame.

"It's just my body," I said, and I smoothed the skin of her cheeks because I thought she might smile, but no, she would not.

It is the time ghost. We understand it now. We make copies of all our legitimate responses to the material world, we see the copies we make the copies from on huge movie screens, loud as hell, or alone with the tiny buds in our ears and the personal screen inches from our face. We have lines to say and whatever we say we know it is the approved expression from a genre we despise, and yet we do feel, we do.

I was alone with my dead wife and shamed, but I dressed her perfectly in her dark skirt and silk blouse the colour of pearls. I had to — after taking a moment away, and looking at the stainless steel cart that held, I guess, instruments and towels and swabs and so on, when it was not in the morgue — had to ask my daughter in from the hallway outside to tell me if I had done a good enough job and she said yes.

My daughter was so lost. She was also doing things correctly and I couldn't think of Helen, myself, not directly, because I didn't know what to do next.

"Not lost," I heard my daughter say, as she spoke to the mortician.

The sudden heat of the summer outside was a lucid moment and I felt there was something kind about its thump. It was thick and a small family walked in the sunshine across the street, a boy in a big hat almost lost behind his mom and dad in the shade of a tree.

My son-in-law was in the driver's seat. My daughter opened the passenger door for me and I got in. When she was in the back seat we started to drive and I told them, "Thank goodness, both of you," and I knew by his glance in the mirror I was still talking gibberish.

"Are you sure you want to speak?" my daughter asked me, and I was sure, though I didn't know what I would say. Even when it's me in the third person, I feel small. Just because I made jokes doesn't mean I didn't believe.

~

"No," he said. "I don't think so."

"It's not that big a deal," she said.

"No, that's true. It's not."

"There are bigger things. This is nothing."

"It's not nothing."

"Okay."

"It isn't."

"Okay. That's true — it's not nothing."

"It's something I care about," he said.

"But in the great scheme — "

"In the great scheme nothing. Don't tell me about the great scheme."

She chewed on a fry, then passed him the ketchup. She finished chewing then pointed the next fry at him, widening her eyes and saying quietly: "Do you deny the existence of The Great Scheme?"

He laughed and said no, no of course not.

"Well?"

"Okay, I get it. Compared to death, compared to pain, torture, so on. I get it."

"This is nothing, right?"

"No, I guess not."

"But you should have started with something else and worked your way up to death."

"What?"

"You said it's nothing compared to death, but you went on, when really you could have stopped there."

"I wanted some volume of things."

"Volume?"

"A list, yes. Maybe a big list."

"Fine, then start with something smaller — "

"Hunger," he said.

"Good one."

"It is."

"Then go from there," she said. "Hunger. Fine. Hunger, then go on to say a broken heart or — "

"Oh Jesus. Here we go."

You Didn't Have to Tell Him

THE SUNSHINE HELD THE PAVEMENT TO the road on our little street. There were big trees around every house, big trees along the sidewalks, but the shade they cast seemed terribly small; barely the space to fit an average yellow dog on the end of its leash, for example, or a dark cat stretching and squinting as if it were lying in front of a fan.

"Nina! I'm going to sit with Mel," I yelled. She was somewhere in the house but I didn't have the time to find her. I paused before I shut the door and really left. I was waiting to hear a response but I didn't. Nina never answered when I was talking about her daddy, even when I didn't use that word. It was her called him Daddy, back when she used to talk about him.

~

He sat in the same booth he always sat in, the one in the back corner nearest the swinging doors to the kitchen. He worked on a puzzle there, in his sweat-stained white shirt. The restaurant had been air-conditioned for ten years now, ever since I moved here, but it was like he stayed hot out of habit; he sweated because he always had.

I love it here on Saturday afternoons precisely because of the air-conditioning. I'm still not used to the heat. I didn't always come just to sit with the old man. Matter of fact, I avoided him most of my married life. But when his mind started to go, I saw love in his eyes. Love is easily misunderstood these days.

"Don't worry, Mr. Hastings," her daddy told me again today. "Summer's almost over."

"Not a day too soon, Mel." I hated it when he called me mister. He always calls me mister. But there is no point in getting your blood up, especially with this one. My own little thing to irritate him, calling him her daddy when they were both grown people, in the end didn't bother him. It bothered me, but I kept on. I've lived my whole life with the feeling I was being watched. I wanted anyone who saw to know I was in on the joke. I don't know if that's about religion.

I sat down in my regular spot, the booth in the far corner away from the kitchen. Her daddy and I can see everyone who's coming in, except he doesn't watch and I get a bit too edgy about the swinging door to the kitchen.

"Now. Life's too short. Don't go wishing it away," Mel said, holding a small piece up to his glasses to study it. He held it there for what seemed like twenty minutes. It wasn't. How could it be?

Eventually, the newest girl came by with a pitcher of water and an empty glass. She set them on my table and brought out her order pad.

"Turkey and gravy on a piece of white toast," I told her, and looked back down to the papers I was marking.

"I had to drop out of your class," she said, and it startled me. I looked up into her face and it did look familiar. She was a pretty, smiling girl with straight black hair. My first impulse was to check her stomach for pregnancy and I'm not sure if that's wrong.

"I'm sorry to hear that," I told her, but she didn't seem too sorry. She laughed and put the pencil in her hair behind her ear, then slid the order pad into the pocket on her short apron. Simple gestures can seem ageless or they can seem ancient. This one was old for a girl like her, and she must have done it a million times since whenever it was she started.

Mel's mind is going, sure, but I am not so sure we all aren't forgetting. My own memory is not perfect. I can't remember the day Nina and I met, for instance — not like Nina can. But I remember the love that I felt the first time we didn't have sex before sleeping together. We were exhausted from our first real jobs and we slept in her bed because her parents were gone on vacation and I had given some story to mine, and it was a Thursday night. She reached over to the nightstand on her side of the bed, got a bottle, and pumped some lotion onto her hands. She lay back and smiled as she rubbed her hands together until all the lotion was gone. It smelled like Fruit Loops. Then she reached over and touched my hand and fell asleep without saying a word. Maybe I only remember it because it was exactly what I thought it was — part of the deep structure of her life, part of her private routine — and she repeats it nightly to this day; but maybe I remember it because it was her being alone with herself for the first time when I was there, and I loved her.

Maybe these simple repeated gestures are all I can understand. This waitress seemed too young to have such a dexterous understanding of the bleak mechanics of her job.

"Yeah," she said. "I didn't want to but I had to drop it. My advisor told me drop one or I might have to drop them all."

She was smiling and I didn't know what to say. Her stomach was showing, it was pointing right at me as she shrugged. That is, it was right at the level of my eye and it was pierced. If she was pregnant she was showing nothing.

"Then where would I be?"

"That would be no good," I said. "You did the right thing."

"Exactly! So then my very next class was your class and we were talking about that story? I forget the name but I loved it."

"What was it about?"

She shook her head and squinted her eyes. She was still smiling, but it was a different smile, more at herself.

I wanted to tell her there's more to life than the name of a story, and there is certainly more to it than the name of an author. The story itself is what matters, but even then, mainly how it moved you, mainly how it made you think. It is about the things suggested in your own life.

But she already knew that, and was trying to hide it out of pity for me, or that's what it seemed like. It did seem like I spent my life remembering names of writers and names of stories, of course. But what she didn't know is that it was a job, like her job.

"I just remember that the woman in the story was trapped and I knew all that on my own. You didn't have to tell me. I knew it. I knew it on my own, before class, I mean."

"Hey, that's good. What do you need me for then, right?"

"Right! Well, I still wanted to take the class but . . . "

"Well, listen," I told her, "those counsellors — "

"Advisors."

" — right, advisors, they know the best way to get the degree you're after."

Her fingers were spread out and touching the edge of the table. They were as thin as the bones at the front of her neck.

"Lived all my life in a college town," Mel said across the room. "Never did go to college."

The girl smiled over at him. He wasn't always way off. He wasn't always in his own world. Sometimes what he said came right from what was going on around him.

"Hey, how's that puzzle coming?" I asked him. The girl and I smiled at each other and we walked together toward the kitchen. Mel's face was huge and open as we approached. He wasn't looking at me. He always liked a pretty smile. He liked girls. I told my wife it was because they smiled more than boys. You should see the way boys treat him. But the girls smile and he doesn't know who they are. He forgets Nina's name sometimes. She doesn't like the way he looks at her then.

"Not too bad. Not too bad," he said as we both turned our attention to the puzzle. There were huge gaps, of course. I couldn't tell how much he'd gotten since last time. But I knew one day he would finish it. Out of the blue it would be done and there would be tears in his eyes and he wouldn't talk to anyone around him. He would just look at the picture on the table in front of him like he was looking at a door that had just been closed. He knew something beautiful was in there, he knew he'd been in there, but how in God's name do you get back?

"You're missing something," I told him, pointing at the biggest gap in the puzzle.

"Well, I never did go to college," he muttered to himself, shuffling the unconnected pieces around on the table. His thick fingers would obliterate a piece just by touching it. "I signed up for the war just out of high school. I just figured, get my two years in and get out."

"But you stayed there twenty-five years."

"But I stayed in twenty-five years. Best thing I ever did."

"You've got money coming in every month."

"I got money coming in every month."

"You're missing most of the cat, here, though, do you see the cat in that pile?"

"Oh, now, she's around the neighbourhood somewhere. Did you see a kitty laying anywhere in the road?"

I thought I might cry when he looked up from the puzzle. What cat? What cat are you thinking about, Mel? This is where I could use her help. What cat is her daddy talking about? He is about to weep over a lost cat from long ago or perhaps imagined and she stays away because he called her the wrong name.

"This orange little cat," I told him, and pointed to a piece of the puzzle. "Here's part of its tail."

"Ha! It is, you son of a bitch! Good for you. Let me take that." And as he did I heard voices at the front door.

~

"You have got to come in the back door," I told the boy, but I shouldn't really joke with them. "We're watching the front door. Somebody's always watching the front door."

The boy didn't flinch. His jaw was tight and he watched someplace behind my skull. I tried to catch his eyes.

"Wherever you go, I mean. Somebody's always watching the front door."

"It isn't right, him just sitting in here like that. He should be put away."

"Wait a minute," I told the boy. I couldn't remember his name, so I asked him.

"Tyler," he said.

"Tyler, he didn't do anything."

"Soon as somebody's not watching, what then?"

"Somebody's always watching."

"Soon as they're not. What then? Soon as somebody falls asleep or gets caught up watching anything else. What then?"

"Tyler, we're all doing our best. That won't happen."

I knew he didn't believe me. I couldn't remember what class I'd taught him. I couldn't remember where I had seen him before, but I knew it was some kind of class.

"What are you up to these days?" I asked him.

In near the doorway the sun played tricks. His glasses glinted so I couldn't really see his eyes. I saw where his eyes would be. I saw movement and shapes there in the sockets, but I also saw some sketch of my reflection, and when I spoke my mouth moved awkwardly; the words didn't match its shape at all.

"You were in a class of mine," I told him. "Which one? I can't remember. Was it just one?"

"It was one."

He stared at me, waiting, but I couldn't remember.

"Do you remember *Of Mice and Men*?" he asked me.

"The book or the movie."

"It doesn't matter," he said, and he turned and left.

These are boys in love with their first real girlfriends. I've stopped trying to explain things to them. They don't like the way Mel looks at their girls. And because the old man moves so slow and they are all speed, he watches them like they're on TV. He comments and he smiles. His vocabulary is shrinking. He remembers small words, crude words that mean the same as big words.

They don't like the things they think they hear him say. They don't like the things he actually says, either.

~

"Maybe they're right," she said, when I got home in the evening. "Maybe there's something to it. What kind of life does he have anyway?"

"What are you talking about?"

"I mean he just does that puzzle. He'll never finish that puzzle."

I pictured her daddy with his oily glasses staring down at the dirty cardboard pieces. He smiled when someone he knew came in. He thought they were coming in to see him, and when he didn't know them, he assumed the same; either way he wanted to be alone with his puzzle.

"He enjoys it, is the thing. What kind of life would he have in a home?"

"He'd sit in his room and do another puzzle. He'd have the same life."

"Not the same. Not the same at all," I said, shaking my head.

"How?"

"Nobody's coming and going in the home. Nobody's coming into his room."

"There's a room they all go to. He could sit there."

I couldn't think of anything to say. Usually I told her we've done it this long, let's keep going. What's the harm? I don't mind and her brother doesn't mind, our nieces and nephews don't mind. I didn't want to bring up her mother. Her mother had died long ago. Part of Nina's problem with her daddy was that her mother died long ago.

"Did anyone come in looking for him today?"

This isn't the kind of question I wanted to answer. There was orange juice in the fridge and I poured some. I took a vitamin because I couldn't remember if I had in the morning. There was some pineapple there on the top shelf, and I wanted it, but couldn't decide if it was worth the sticky mess it would make on my hands. It would get on my chin and then onto my shirt, too. I had to bite into it. I couldn't help it. I couldn't put a whole piece in my mouth no matter how small it was. It was too sweet. I needed air in there too.

"Yeah. They're just worried about nothing."

"How do you know?"

"He never did a thing that you know of, right?"

"I see the way he looks at girls sometimes."

"He likes the way they smile," I told her. "They smile at him."

"Not all of them," she said. "He doesn't even remember who I am. He forgets I'm his daughter."

"He never sees you anymore. Where would he remember you from?"

She didn't speak and I didn't want to continue. It was the wrong thing to say. I had said the wrong thing.

"I'm sorry, Helen. He knows you sometimes. He talks to me all the time about you. He remembers when you were a child. He never touched you then, right?"

"Of course not."

She stood watching me from the other side of the kitchen island. I closed the fridge and turned to smile at her. What had happened to her? There were a million things I could think of, but didn't want to. Why wouldn't she tell me?

Her hands were brown and the fingers turned white at their tips as she pushed them down on the counter. Her hair was tied back but one dark strand hung down on the left of her face. Her bottom lip jutted out slightly when she was thinking.

I remember the first time I noticed she dyed her hair. It was ages ago but she isn't that old. It was over a year after we moved in together and I was proud of her for keeping it from me for so long. What an odd thing to be proud of, but I was. She was on her knees behind the house, planting something beside the patio. I walked up silently behind her and knelt there. She kept her hair short then and I saw the smallest edge of grey at her roots as I kissed her neck.

I hadn't surprised her, of course. And what I was proud of wasn't that she fooled me, because she hadn't. What I admired about her as she planted all sorts of colours in the sun around our new house, was that she still had something that was just her own. I tried to keep secrets but I couldn't. I told her everything I knew, every day.

"Remember that first house?" I asked her there in the kitchen.

"Of course," she said, but she wasn't in the mood. "Yes. Yes, I remember that house. It was great. It was fine."

"He's still your daddy," I told her, even though I hadn't meant to.

"That doesn't change a thing. You say that every time."

"Just 'cause you don't see him, or just 'cause you don't call him that."

"You say that every time."

She's right. I say that every time.

~

On Monday I'll try to get her daddy out of the booth. He'll curse me and ask me why can I never leave him alone, just leave him to it.

"You're so goddam jealous of me it makes me sick," he bellows. "Every one of them girls — you can't stand it 'cause you're an old man."

When I start to push him gently toward the door, the pain and exertion from his shuffling take over. He tells me life is hell and don't ever get old.

His eyes get wilder and wetter as we get to the door.

"I just want to finish that goddam puzzle," he hisses as I push him out into the world. Once he hauls himself up the step from the sidewalk to the barber shop, once he's balanced again, he sees Ernie and smiles.

He grows and straightens out as he puts his hat and coat on the rack. He stands like he's ready for anything that comes.

"My son-in-law, Ernie," he says, gesturing toward me.

"Never catch me chumming around with my wife's daddy."

"Well, we're all grownups here, Ernie. When he first came sniffing around I didn't much like him. But what can you do? He turned out pretty good."

~

The kinds of things Mel says are okay in the barbershop most times. I take him on a weekday, just in case, when usually there are no mothers and children in there. Ernie doesn't take offense. Talking's just talking, anyway.

Well if you get in there and ask the wrong question he'll go on a tear. He never got hired at the plant, back when there was one, because of what people thought of him. That was back when the plant was running and back before Ukrainians were white. He gave coal away to the women in the '30s when he was working for the railway. He'd walk along the tops of the cars and throw it down to the women, who would gather it in their aprons. To hear him tell it he could've been in Marvel comics with the Sub-Mariner or Sgt. Fury, only he was winning the war at home, standing atop a high-speed train dispensing coal to the peasants as the rich industrialists tried to stop him. That's one thing I loved about him; it was a war, that one. He was right.

I've heard all these stories, though, so I mostly sit and look out the glass front of the barber shop. We get him a shave, too, and Ernie takes his time.

People walk by now and then on the sidewalk. Their faces are hidden unless the shadow of a cloud passes over and darkens the scene; then we can all see everything from where we sit on the wine-coloured chairs. I am always surprised when the unbearable lightness breaks into shade and someone walks by with a smile. The shapes without faces seem angry.

Old guys have their hands stuffed in their pockets, even on hot days. Unless they're like Mel, then they need them out and ready to hold onto some kind of building or rail, just in case.

We go right to his little room above the restaurant. He sits way back in his chair and rubs the back of his neck.

"That son of a bitch does a good job," he says.

Just once, she could come by, and see her daddy talking to Ernie. She could be one of those people walking up the sidewalk, listening to the world around her, smiling at something somebody said. She could help me bring him home after his haircut, all shined up and feeling fine. He breathes deeply and has all sorts of plans. He's got no time for the puzzle. Let's get out to the track, he'll say. I feel lucky.

Make the Soup

YOU BUILD THE FACTORY. YOU MAKE the soup the workers eat. You build a house about twenty minutes by bus from the factory. The bus route doesn't matter to the story; all you need is twenty minutes from end to end. Those twenty minutes work either way, whether the line is crooked or straight. All you need are the facts:

A factory.

A house.

The boy's father works at the factory and it takes him twenty minutes to get there, twenty minutes to get home at night.

Now the man's got a son, but not a wife. Why doesn't he drive? Why doesn't he have a wife?

The boy's got red hair and pale skin. He sits tapping at his computer at night, inventing reasons his father's alone. He's got a good imagination. It could be any number of things.

1) His mother died in the car crash that hurt his father's eye. It takes care of the driving. It takes care of the wife.

2) His father never needed nothing that wasn't on the bus route anyway, so . . . Safeway, the little branch of the city library, the walk-in clinic, the Credit Union, etc. . .

3) But those twenty minutes he is on the bus. The boy knows his father has ten minutes at the factory before his job starts, and ten minutes waiting for the bus on the way home. In those ten minutes each way, ten minutes twice each day, anything can happen. Women must work in the factory too. Women must take the bus.

4) His father must have had all he would ever need with the boy's mother. Her name was Linda, and she cooked exotic food. Nobody ever went hungry before she died. There was hot clear soup and creamy thick soup. There was homemade bread, fresh vegetables from the garden, and his father smiled. He took the bus to work because his mother needed the car to do good things all day — search for ingredients, feed the homeless downtown.

5) Now there are three closets filled with no-name vegetables, soups, and fruit. Nobody starves even though the mother is dead.

6) The women at the factory see the boy's father but maybe to them he has too big a belly, though he has no belly at all. Maybe to them his teeth are not straight, though only one at the bottom is out of place. Maybe to them he is just a short man with a skinny pale son.

7) The boy looks in the mirror every day. He is too thin. His hair is too red. On his mother that red was beautiful. He is so pale he feels blue.

8) The women at the factory seem shy. They see his father and have heard of his mother. Who am I beside this beautiful ghost? they think. I am too thick in the middle. I am too wrinkled near my eyes and my smile seems childish compared to her smile in that picture he keeps in the living room.

9) That's if they had come home with him one time on the bus. Perhaps it was when the boy stayed out on a winter night, working on the yearbook at school, knowing that if you take the pictures no one looks at you.

10) That time his father didn't snore in his chair while the hockey game played. He sat on the couch beside the woman from work. She was powdered and fresh and he had just parted his hair. They drank rye and Coke from plastic glasses.

11) The boy can't imagine this. Did he hear laughter the next morning from the kitchen? Is that how his mother sounded? This woman was likely too thoughtless to be like his mother. His mother's laugh must have been the kind that could never be mistaken for mocking.

12) The kind of laughter that one hides behind walls shouldn't be so spring-like. It shouldn't bounce up out of the still morning, as his mother's might have. Not if it's going to be loud and wake him up. He trusts himself when he's sleeping — if he was startled, then it's because something was startling.

13) He can't remember if he was startled or if he woke slowly, smiling, and then was startled when the dream wasn't true.

14) Then there is no factory. The bus route changes and the boy's father doesn't take the bus. On the days when he leaves the house, he walks. He's got all the time in the world. He leaves early and walks downtown. It takes almost an hour.

15) In this hour, once a week, he may meet anyone at all. Maybe one of the ladies from work lives along his way. She sees him coming and times perfectly her entrance through

her front gate onto the public sidewalk. Hello, she says. Hello, Miss, he says, and they both smile. They speak quite nicely to each other. You are beautiful, his father even says, and she can tell by the light in his eyes that he means it.

16) The unemployment office is hard on blossoming romances and a couple of things can happen. Maybe one of them gets another job. There is no need for the long walks. They decide they will meet anyway, in the evenings or on the weekends, but the first time is too awkward. Nobody is asking for a handout, but one wants to talk about work and one wants to talk about hoping to work.

17) I will make you dinner, the woman says, but she knows the man will not walk all that way for a handout. It's not a handout, because she wants to whisper to the man when they're alone, and she would prefer to go to his house and eat there. She could meet the boy. They could see how it goes. But it never goes further, and the boy and the woman don't meet. This is probably a mistake.

18) What's more likely, because his father could get a job if the woman could — his father knows almost everything there is to know, you should see his books, you should hear the answers he tells the TV — what's more likely is the woman did not want to keep walking. It came to be winter and the bus went right by them. Let's take it, she'd say. But the boy's father is far-sighted. He knows what money is worth when there is none. He knows it's worth less when there is some. He knows nothing lasts, and anything can happen (look at the factory and how it is gone when all the people still buy the things that the factory made, and he reads in the paper how much money they make), so as long as his legs last he will use them.

19) She used to look sadly at the man in the street as she whisked by on the bus. She couldn't speak to him at the Unemployment Office because she felt sorry for him — a man like that must drink his money away, or at least he'd be able to afford the bus. She decides it is best for everyone.

20) Or maybe the woman said her name was Linda, the first time she came out onto the sidewalk. His father is a decent man. He tried to be friendly. I can't be in love with two Lindas, he thought. Linda was the boy's mother. Next thing you know she'll be in the kitchen, trying to make soup. Next thing you know she'll be in the boy's room. She won't have red hair and she'll be looking over his shoulder saying what's this you're typing? Why aren't I in the story? Why don't you come with us out into the sunshine?

21) The boy's father wouldn't let the fake Linda make the boy do anything he didn't want to. Whoever named you was mistaken, he would type, as this confused woman looked over his shoulder, you're not Linda at all.

Whose Origin Escaped Him

PETE WALKED INTO THE KITCHEN AND, without turning on the light, opened the cupboard and pulled out a coffee mug.[1] He put the white mug on the counter; one side was slightly pink in the light of the red digital clock at the gurgling coffee maker's base.[2] Out of habit, he looked out the kitchen window as he walked to the fridge for the cream.[3] Once at the fridge, he opened its door and stared inside, forgetting what he was there for.[4] He stared at the cream, then took it out, pushing the top edges backwards, which accordioned the ragged wet mouth of the carton open in a tired diamond, then he poured himself a little cream,

[1]The character Pete is unlikely to die, though stranger things have happened. In an earlier version of this story, Pete did die. In that case I felt an obligation to warn the reader, so he or she would not feel cheated. If Pete is unlikely to die, perhaps no comment is warranted.

[2] Here you expect the time, which is 4:34 AM, to be mentioned, though it is not. There is also no need to explain how the coffee is made already, with the lights off, and Pete presumably just waking up.

[3]This habit is from summer days, when he can see the trees outside. Maybe the birds are feeding. But he holds onto the habit in the winter because he also gets comfort from seeing his own reflection in the dark window. It is difficult to see, because all the lights are off, but he is practiced at picking his own form out of the dark. He feels, on most days, a kind of familial warmth as this character briefly appears.

[4]His forgetfulness is, each time, for a different reason. Suppose on this day the form his reflection took in the window was a clue — it was too youthful or too old. It reminded him of an event in the past, or a worry for the future. Or suppose it had something to do with the present day, something to do with his tasks now, as a person in his kitchen, with a day of work to get to.

returned the carton to the fridge and closed the fridge door.[5] He took his coffee out of the kitchen, through a short hallway, and into another room.[6]

Turning on his computer, Pete stared at the screen, waiting for it to go through its startup routine.[7] He picked up a scrap of paper and read the writing on it; this quotation he had been searching for, he could not get it out of his head, but what was the origin?[8] He needed the information and would google it again, for the one-hundredth time.[9]

[5] It's impossible to let this go without comment. Notice how Pete becomes irrelevant as the narrator tries to be literary? Did she really make this character, name him Pete, give him a house and a partner, simply to describe him opening a box of cream?

Knowing human nature as I do does not help me understand this narrator. I have travelled throughout North America with a listening ear and open eyes. Things I've seen have been impossibly difficult and sad. Never mind. I don't yet know how my own life will turn out.

I thought of having Pete write an elegy. I thought of telling the whole story through his sweaty flight to Edmonton. He wants to keep his ego out of it. He is afraid to fall in love with the sound of his own tears, or their shape, and it hurts him to turn red at a typo while delivering his elegy. He knows the only death especially about him is his own.

[6] It will be clear, I hope, that the next room is his office. This room is a mess. There is one table with a computer on it. Beside the table is a filing cabinet and on the opposite wall two short shelves of books. The floor is covered with papers, loosely fitting the form of "stacks." The impression is that at one time the furnishings had been chosen to give the office a spare, clean feeling — but Pete has been unable to maintain this feeling. This room is a mess, but the mess doesn't extend to the house beyond. A door may be closed on this room and for Pete and his partner that is enough.

This morning as he sits down and turns his computer on, he has to move a scrap of paper from beside the mouse in order to set his coffee down. On this paper are the words "It's midnight for the prairie hero." Beside these words are less readable letters that ask "Where is this line from?" and more letters that say "FIND OUT."

[7] Possibly this is the closest thing to tension that we will find in Pete's story: what is he turning this on for? Will this be enough? Maybe not. Maybe you are the only one still reading.

[8] If I were Pete, I would be as lost as he is. I have put bits of my own life in here to help me relate to him. There are things he says which I have said, and so on.

[9] Pete is not omniscient. The narrator could use her own omniscience to spell out the exact number of times he has googled it, but that sort of authorial intrusion quickly detracts from the gritty realism of this slice-of-life narrative. At least it does to me, when I read books like this.

(But, since we are here, it goes like this: he has been searching for this quotation for eight days, with a two-day break in there where he and his partner travelled to Edmonton in order to attend a funeral that was ridiculously unexpected. Pete could

The phone rang and Pete picked it up and listened for a minute.

"I know that," he said.

While he continued to listen, the computer finished its startup routine and he thought he might change his desktop.[10]

"I know," he said, and hung up the phone.

He shook his head, rubbed his eyes, then turned the picture on the left side of his desk face down.[11] He stood the picture back up and looked at it.[12] He moved it as far as he could to the left side of his desk, then turned it to face the door of his little office.[13]

He stretched his back, pushing his arms up and away from his body, slowly opening his fists and spreading his fingers as far as they would spread.[14] Then he shuddered

---

have googled it while at the hotel in Edmonton but the emotional toll this sudden death took on all of them would not allow it. In fact, it is only the deadline he faces, here, today, that has him back at it so early. So that means six days (not counting today because it is just beginning and the computer has yet to finish its startup routine). Each of those six days began with a google search and there were between nine and seventeen throughout the day. Every possible way of stringing these words together has been attempted ("It's midnight for the prairie hero"; It's-midnight-for-the-prairie-hero; and so on) for a total of seventy-three searches.)

[10]His desktop is unlikely to change in the course of this story. It is a grey picture of the sky somewhere. At the top left there is a sentence: "We must love one another or die." In the middle of the screen, the sentence has been emended: "We must love one another and die." At the bottom right, there is no sentence. All three are from Auden.

[11]In this photo, he and his sister smile beside his aging mother. Thankfully, his mother was gone by the time his sister died.

[12]It is impossible to judge. Here, he looks unmoved. He looks as if the people in the photo are unknown to him, but I am sure he is not cold. I know he is moved because of the time this takes. There is a period of at least thirty seconds which is unaccounted for by the narration, and during that time he thinks many things, like he wished he still smoked, like why does this deadline matter, like why it does matter, like did his sister say anything at the end and how did they know to call him?

[13]This way anyone can see it when they walk by in the hallway, if they are moving between the bathroom and the kitchen or the living room, say. Also, he does not have to see it today, at least, while he works to the deadline.

[14] I cannot separate his actions this morning from my own. He needs some kind of physical release. He needs to be free of his heart and feel something other than grief.

almost imperceptibly and smiled.[15] With his body loose he took a sip of his coffee and stared at his desktop.[16] After returning his cup to his desk, he let his hand rest on the phone.[17] Breathing deeply, he picked the receiver up and hit a speed dial button.[18]

"Hi. Sorry," he said. After a slight pause he continued: "I can't find it. I just don't know where it is."[19]

He closed his eyes and listened to the voice on the other end of the line.[20]

"Well, I can't. If I don't know where it is, it can't be in the book. We need permission."[21]

---

[15] I understand this also. A smile is a physiological response, similar to tears, or a sneeze. When I was younger I would have doubted the significance of this. I would not have noticed. As the years pass, I feel more and more like an old man apologizing for stains left behind.

It's just like here, right now, with Pete. Before his smile is finished he feels guilt, remembering his surprise and his sorrow at his sister's death. What the smile means is he is glad to be alive, which on some level he takes to mean this absurd universe has made the right decision. He concurs. But before the smile is over he disagrees, and wants again to forget his body and its simple response to each little heartbeat.

[16] This is precisely the occasion the Auden lines were meant for, I think. Though Pete is still angry at Auden for leaving the line out in the final version.

[17] When I got the news of a loved one's sudden death via the phone, I wanted to have that phone with me no matter what for the next few days. I kept it on the top of the back of the toilet as I showered. I held it when I was on the street, so that I wouldn't miss any possible call of retraction. I was afraid the sounds of the street — the various languages, the irrational pings and gongs from the sculptor working down on the beach, the laughter of those odd little men who met each other every morning outside the Bread Garden — would somehow synchronize with the ring tone of my phone, and be unheard. In most cases that synchronicity might be enough to convince me there is order in this world, but in this case I needed, instead, my brother never to have died.

[18] He is calling his partner. It's not that his partner is intended to be male and the ambiguity may make the story more accessible to heterosexuals. It's also not that his partner is a woman and the ambiguity is meant to show their non-gendered equality. It is just that, right now, it does not matter. Pete wants to press his head to the forehead of the person he loves for the same reason he would lie on the cool unfinished concrete after a long day at work in the sun as a teenager.

[19] The quotation he is looking for. "It's midnight for the prairie hero."

[20] Perhaps Pete's partner responds more to his unstated grief than to the issue of the quotation.

[21] It's already very late in the process. Pete's publisher needs permission for the use of the quotation. Pete has just finished a western with Leonard Cohen as his hero. It's

With the thumb and first finger of his left hand he rubbed his eyes through their closed lids as he listened.[22]

"I need it in the book. It makes sense. But the editor can't find it either. Even if I find it, it's probably too late."

Still listening, he stood up from his chair and, without opening his eyes, lay down on his back on the floor, his closed eyes staring straight up.[23]

"I guess."

It was as if he was sleeping, and his left eye leaked; a wet line ran from its corner down his cheek.[24] He only felt it when it hit his ear.[25]

"When I think about it I suppose nothing depends upon it. It's not an imagist poem."[26]

He breathed deeply then opened his eyes.[27] From his vantage point on the floor he looked up at the window. He couldn't remember how much he would see from here, if it wasn't dark; not much, he thought, because he couldn't see even one star.[28]

---

called *Listen All You Bullets*, and the line "It's midnight for the prairie hero" is in a book in the story, and functions as a refrain repeated by the little boy in the last chapter.

[22] On the other end of the line, words are repeated. Pete has heard them before, as recently as last night when he was trying his best to fall asleep. The basic message is: *but you* need *it in the book. It's* integral. *It is the* metafictive lynchpin.

[23] *It is not the end of the world if that line is not included. It may be a different story, but only slightly. It will be the same story, differently told.*

[24] He doesn't bother with certain things anymore, such as wiping his eyes when these odd tears roll out. It's not a function of his emotional state, but simply a matter of getting old and not worrying about anybody seeing anything. He knows how little attention he really attracts, especially when alone in his house.

[25] Normally in this case he may rub his ear, but not now. He is too intent on the words coming from the phone: *It won't, really, change anything. The beauty of these stories is how far they're removed from that dependence on traditional emotional strategies.*

[26] He is referring, of course, to the William Carlos Williams poem. We all supply our own meaning here. Something depends upon our tenuous connection to the grand scheme outdoors. We don't know what it is, but we may die for lack of it.

[27] He heard things like *I'm sorry* and *the story* and *don't worry*; things that vaguely rhymed and all ran together.

[28] Pete has never looked in this direction before. He has never been in this position. He is mistaken about the stars — that is no measure at all, since outside it is overcast.

"The story will survive without it. I know. I don't know why it seems like such a big deal."[29]

"Thanks," he said finally and turned the phone off. It rang again.

"No," Pete said. "Take the boy out of the story." [30]

"Mm hmmn."

"I'm getting another call."

"The boy stays in the story," I said. [31] "Look around."

---

[29] Actually, Pete should not worry; the line in question is from one of his own poems. If he went through the stack of old little magazines in the northwest corner of his office, he would find a small mimeographed journal called *Hostbox*. On page 14 of issue 9, is a poem called "Prairie Realism," which ends with the line "but it's night time for the prairie hero" — not quite what he remembered, but close enough.

[30] I said he should not worry.

[31] The boy is already *in* the story. His inability to say what you want him to say means nothing.

Big Books Shut

"GENTLEMEN," I SAID, "I HAVE TO be going."

The one holding my hat appeared puzzled. The dark-haired one with the sharp face punched me again in the ribs. His tiny hand was hard but there was little force behind the blow. One of those holding me chuckled.

"Wait," said the boy with my hat.

"What?" the dark one asked.

"Let's hear what he has to say," he said, putting one hand on the small boy's shoulder.

"We don't listen to them," the one holding my left arm said.

"They don't usually talk."

At that, both of the boys holding my arms let go. There were four of them altogether: the two larger ones had been holding my arms; the leader was holding my hat; and the little dark-haired boy was in charge of harassing and hurting me.

I tried to tidy myself up a bit, to smooth wrinkles from my shirt, for instance, and straighten my tie, but it was little use; the altercation had made me quite grubby.

"My hat please, sir," I said, and held out my hand.

"We certainly don't give back hats," the boy said, and smiled. The others chuckled and I was taken by how the boy seemed to grow with the laughter. His silver tooth was a charming irregularity, not ugly at all.

"Of course," I said, and bent down to tie my shoe. And the shoe was still tied, mind you. I looked up at the ring-leader, the silver-toothed boy with my hat. "As I say, I've got to be going."

"Of course," the little dark-haired one said, preparing to kick me.

But I had, by then, taken my knife from my sock, and, as usual, all the boys ran away as soon as one of them was stabbed.

"Some of us have guns," I told the boy. "You're lucky." This little man who was all bravado looked around quickly for his playmates and then began to cry. He clutched his wounded side and tried to stop the tears, or at least the sound of them.

"I'm on my way to the hospital anyway," I said. "We'll share a cab."

~

"You should have left him," the taxi driver said. "He's a filthy rat. He'll die soon enough anyway. At least if he dies today he will do no more harm."

"Nonsense," I said. "He is little. And now he is alone. And afraid."

I slapped the boy's hand away. I told him the knife would come out when we got to the hospital. There are regulations. He chattered and whined about the cold, but I told him he was only in shock, not actually cold. Besides, the window, in all fairness to the taxi driver, must remain down while I smoked. The boy screamed at me, almost hysterical.

"Seriously," I told him. "Shut up and let me relax. I am on my way to my volunteer work."

"What is it you do?" the driver asked, waiting for the light to turn green.

"Backrubs and so on."

"The freeloaders?"

"That's right."

"My father was a freeloader at the end. Finally, he took care of it himself. He had principles."

"Ha! We all do, of course. But I know what you mean. Some of us have principles that are absolute. We are not taken in by the soft world around us. Pleasure and so on."

Birds pecked the ground between the cab and the shop on the left side of the street. What could they be looking for? The sealed surface of the world offered no place for seeds. The youth leaves trash on the ground, of course, and some of it is eaten by birds.

"There will be a new paradigm," the driver said. "As early as next year."

"I don't doubt it, but nothing will change."

The driver shrugged and we got going as the light changed.

"I don't know what you guys are talking about," the boy said through his chattering teeth.

"I told you shut up," I said. "You've got a knife in you. Conserve your energy."

"About the blood . . . " the driver said, looking at me in his rear-view mirror.

"It's fine," I told him. "I have a form."

"Of course." He nodded.

~

"But you are old," I said. "Your life is of little value."

The old man was almost sleeping. His spotted skin sprouted hairs here and there, some wiry and thick, others light as an idea of hair. His breathing sounded like snoring and his back was bony. The skin moved inches as I kneaded — it was like the stockings that hang like shed snakeskin around some women's thick and veined ankles.

"I say your life is of little value, because of your age," I told him, leaning down to his ear.

"I heard you, goddammit! I'm getting a backrub. Keep quiet and let me enjoy it." He relaxed immediately. He didn't care if my response was positive or negative. He spoke and assumed that was the end of it.

"I am the very one rubbing your back," I said to him.

He just lay there.

I removed my hands from his back and watched him. His breathing changed slightly and a small snore came from his enormous nose crammed into the pillow.

"Listen, Pop," I told him, shaking him awake. "I've stopped your backrub."

"All right. Goodbye."

The man was infuriating. I had been making conversation. I did not have to do that. I was under no obligation to befriend anyone. No obligation at all.

What I was trying to tell him was this: Your life is worth nothing, right? It's worth nothing until I come by with a camera and take photos or movies. I create a document somehow, showing "this hideous old creature, etc."

~

But, the freeloaders don't listen. They lie there and expect. They expect and they sometimes get what they expect.

My father years ago told me not to expect. It only means you think you know what's coming next, and you don't. Hüsker Dü. That's how he used to talk. He would say something, quote somebody I had never heard of, then say their name quickly in a quieter voice. Hüsker Dü was a band, he told me. Post-post-something. My father.

His room was cold then, and my father sat in a chair under blankets, watching the television news. So this is the end, he said. I never would have thought. They have taken my blood. I am now using blood by such and such corporation. I am breathing air by Petro-Canada, and so on.

I took the garbage out for him. I would open the windows, and, later, turn up the heat.

You can afford this, I said.

Why should I have to, he said.

There were back-and-forths, that is to say. It went like that.

Jesus, get some clothes on, I would say when I finally got the blanket off him.

I was wearing that blanket, you asshole.

~

I don't remember what my crime was. I don't know if I am still committing it. I have often been in trouble for wearing my hat. It's a brown hat. A hat of light brown leather. The leather is raw and worn, the colour of butterscotch, the colour of fine silt that has baked in the sun and is beginning to welcome the first drops of rain. It's a soft leather hat, and it has a bendable brim around it. It used to be called a cowboy hat. Some cowboy. Some hat. Winston Churchill.

Ten years ago I walked into a bank, wearing this hat. I didn't see the signs.

Of course, the signs were there. Ignorance is not a defense. Tell that to everyone you meet. It's a valuable lesson.

PLEASE REMOVE HATS AND SUNGLASSES FOR SECURITY REASONS

Something happened at the bank that day. I never found out exactly what. They watched the whole story unfold on the security tapes and I was the only unusual character there.

I didn't argue, really. I told my lawyer right off the bat I would plead guilty to wearing the hat. It's not the hat, he said. It's the money. It's the money that disappeared while you wore the hat.

I know that, I told him, I was joking. He didn't appreciate the humour.

Halfway through our discussion I realised this wasn't my lawyer. He was a lawyer for the Crown. This is an odd world. I had been saving money to escape somewhere. My father was recently deceased and there were parts of the world that appealed to me — there were sections of the coast up north, for instance, where all you might see is this white earth, where in summer you would need a hat or die somehow from the sun that never set.

Do you have the money? the lawyer asked and I nodded.

Fair enough. It cost me that much, but I wasn't in jail. I was sentenced to community service. I have a certain fondness for freeloaders of all kinds, so it worked out. As I say, my father was a freeloader. The taxi driver's father was a freeloader who could not bear it, and did himself in.

When I heard that, there in the cab, I could not help but compare it to my own father's situation. Later, near the end, especially. I bought him soft pajamas that went on and off easily. He was barely aware of his surroundings.

The air outside his window was alive with birds, and their words. I held the cloth as he blew his nose. He watched the birds. He looked for them in his limited range of vision, without moving his head, as I held the cloth to his nose. He watched them and smiled as I wiped his nose. I rubbed ointment on his red and chapped nostrils and all the while his hands were folded at his waist, on top of his covers.

These are symbols of birds, he told me. We can't think of them as having families and relationships. At least I can't, anyway. I see one blue jay in the frame of my vision and I think it's the same one that left my sight ten minutes ago. Even if I see two, I think of them as a pair, not as two birds possibly unrelated.

I didn't know what to say. I listened to him go on about birds. It was the only thing outside the room he cared about.

The hands that held each other lightly on top of his stomach strained lightly sometimes, as if they were dreaming of old gestures. Wild animals dreaming about the way they used to chase the air.

~

This boy you brought in has died, they told me.

"Forms to fill out, I guess," I said, laughing.

The woman who told me this wore a white suit. Very official. She nodded because no words were needed. Very good. The slip she handed me had a room number on it. She turned to leave.

"What about my knife?" I asked.

"Go to the room," she said, and was gone. The entire enterprise had taken one minute. Perhaps she had other work. Surely distribution of these slips of paper was not her only task. The long hallway I was in had many doors. It was practically empty, except for the odd chair.

~

The room on the slip was just off a kind of foyer, and outside its door there was a long table. A container of knives was on the table.

In fact, my knife was not in the plastic bin. Most of these were casual knives — knives not for killing, or fighting, necessarily, but knives that must have been close at hand when an incident or idea sparked their wielders to slice or stab. In the bin were also two flat-headed screwdrivers.

"My knife is not in there," I explained to the clerk who sat behind the table. The clerk was oblivious to me, reading his beat-up library book. He was intent upon finishing the current chapter or verse.

I waited a moment, rocking slightly back and forth on my feet, my hands politely clasped behind my back. I heard breathing, or the rhythmic rustling of sheets, or maybe a breeze pushing quietly through the screen of an open window. There was a light curtain across the doorway behind the clerk's desk. Perhaps he was a kind of receptionist for whatever went on through the doorway — inspections or treatments or people lying quietly to recover, or take a turn for the worse.

"My knife is not there," I repeated.

The clerk looked up at me, pushing the chair away from the desk. "You better double-check," he said, standing and stretching, straining his hands toward the ceiling. "Listen, bud," he said. "Did you ever hear about what used to be here?"

"Sir, I did not. Now, I must be retrieving my knife."

"You haven't double-checked," he said. "Now. This place, this very site, was once a primitive garden, I think."

I looked at the slightly damp forehead of the young man. Perhaps his chubbiness is what made him sweat. His watch strap cut slightly into the soft flesh near his wrist. He might have tried harder to appear official. He was a clerk and doing nothing but reading a book. He might address people more properly.

"You might know this, chief," he said, suddenly showing interest in me. "What were those things? You know those things where they grew things. I know garden is wrong but you know those plants they have now?"

I knew what he meant, though I had never been near one. There are stacked drawers of synthetic soil. They contain power and light and water. They are stacked around the hydro plants, producing foods.

"They were called farms," I said to him, taking a deep breath. Surely he and I were together on one thing — he worked here and so did I, though in differing capacities and for different reasons. "Now, let's address the matter of my knife. I will take it and complete the appropriate forms. If necessary, after my work with the freeloaders tomorrow, I can return to your department."

The word department seemed to make him smile and he looked around the foyer, yawning, and pointed again to the plastic bin of knives.

~

Now, there is the question of my knife, where is it and so on, but there is also the question of this man who will no longer talk to me. Things are different in this world than they used to be, I agree. But it is much more than the way we get our food. It's the rules we have invented for ourselves. It's the rules we are given to live under. Rules we know or don't know by habit and do not question.

What is stopping me, for instance, from walking right past this man and into the back room, the room that is hidden by the sheet, or curtain, over the doorway?

He has no gun.

I'm in trouble with the law already, really — witness my daily work with the freeloaders. He has only an old-fashioned telephone on his desk to communicate with the other security types. But the time it would take, to punch in the numbers, to have it ring somewhere else, to have it answered by exactly the person he needed to answer it — surely that would take longer than this man would need to subdue a man like me?

Especially if he is some kind of martial arts expert.

But he seems reasonable. Perhaps he would listen to reason.

Or perhaps he would begin with the terrible windpipe-crushing hold and move on to reason from there.

But why would I stand and wait for my knife while he ignores me? Why is this the sort of rule I would follow?

These are the rules I am talking about. I have emerged somehow, this day, into a world where I am expected to abide by all these agreements made in my absence or even with my tacit approval, given only perhaps by my not screaming *no* and refusing the smallest encroachment on my rights sometime years ago. And that may have been only my right to not accept a discount, say, offered by some political group that did not represent itself as political at all

~

"This was once some kind of open space," the clerk said, taking his watch off and rubbing where it had been. He looked at me while he rubbed. He continued to look at me as he clasped his watch-strap together again and laid it on the table.

"Where?" I asked, because he continued to stare at me as if waiting for some kind of answer, though he hadn't asked a question. This was once some kind of open space — what kind of a question is that? That's not a question.

"Right here," he said, smiling and opening his arms. "Right here. That's the thing about it. It was once all open. It was all an open space and everything lived in the open air."

"It sounds fantastic," I said.

"I bet it was."

"Now, I have to be going. Perhaps you can help me find my knife?"

"I would like to," he said, sitting down and returning his attention to the book he had been reading.

"Why don't you?"

But he didn't answer. He was smiling into his book and he was the kind of guy, he really was the kind of guy who could do only one thing at a time, I suppose, so I reached over and put my hand on his shoulder.

He swatted my hand away and looked up at me surprised.

"I need to find my knife," I told him, but just then the phone on his desk rang. He held his hand out to me with its palm open as he picked up the phone. I suspected it was someone calling from just behind him, from the doorway he was guarding.

~

I turned from the man, rather than look into his pudgy palm. This could be anywhere, I thought. Of course, I had never been to this part of the hospital before, but I was amazed by the plain empty corridor. There were no chart boxes on the walls by the doors. There must be people through the doors, and these would be sick and sleeping or worried and waiting or simply doctors sorting through files or scribbling notes or entering data and slamming big books shut.

My father had been in just such a building, in the end, but was I imagining things or did the buildings used to be full? Was there not bustling, in those days? Were people not brushing past you, barely looking up from the clipboards in their hands?

Now there is no one about.

I turned back to the clerk, but he was gone. The phone was hung up and the man was gone. The book he was reading was on the desk, face down. The cover simple: one of those once-elegant cream-coloured hardcovers that is part of a series of great books. I picked it up. The title was centred on both the front and the back: *As For Me and My House.* Never heard of it. I was aware of the sound of my own breathing. I was alone with this bin of knives and the doorway behind the clerk's desk.

Fair is fair. I will get my own knife, I thought, and stepped past the table. At the curtain I stopped and looked around. What kind of crime would I be committing by entering? There is no way to tell. In the old days, there were signs everywhere you looked. Even if you ignored them, there were still signs.

There was no sound of footsteps.

~

When I entered the room, I relaxed and forgot the clerk. The room was a shambles, you might say, and surely the man at the desk bore some responsibility for that. His credibility was severely diminished right then. I was certain he neglected his work to read his great book and ask questions about things that happened a long time ago. Things that had nothing to do with us now.

There were two large sinks in the far right corner of the room. There were cots on wheels pushed into the far left corner and these cots were covered with sheets and straps and pans of instruments. Perhaps my knife had been lost among the piles of cloth and metal pans.

Somebody was breathing in amongst the pile. It was a raspy sound like wind through fabric, but it was a breath, I was sure. I thought it might be the fat clerk, hiding for a nap. This is what I was thinking. This is what stress can do to you.

I yanked the top sheet and heard a small yelp. Soon I had the young man uncovered. He was naked and holding a knife. It was my knife and this was the boy, looking at me, unsurprised, just taking it all in. Nothing could shock him.

It was all he could do to manage his physical pain and nothing else would move him. He was watching his own final moments and did not care. It isn't did not care, he probably welcomed the end, that's what pain will do to you.

My own father had a lucid moment toward the end of his life. It was only a week or so before he died. He could barely move but I read to him and sometimes he would smile. One night I had my ear down to his mouth to hear what he had to say, if anything, and he strung together many words in a row. It was a big moment, talking to my dad for the first time in many days. He told me this was no way to live, no sense to it, he was too drugged, he could not enjoy it, it was not living, and so on. I told him I knew what he meant but how could I? The pain would be too much.

I can handle the pain, he said. This is too much, this fog, there is one thing left for me to do and I won't even know when I do it. He looked at me and I have to believe he was unable to say what he wanted. I have to believe it was physical, or brought on by the drugs — what happened.

He told me, "You are not the son I imagined," and then went on muttering. I didn't understand his mutterings. And this little conversation was the cause of one of my greatest regrets. Because of it, I lessened the dose of his medication. He wanted off altogether but I just lessened it.

I woke in the night to check on him and he was not screaming or thrashing about but, on closer inspection, was gritting his teeth and sweating and holding on so hard to the rails of the bed I thought they might snap off.

I made some minor conversation with him then, as I washed his forehead and neck with a cool wet cloth, and he tried his best to smile. How far can we take this? I asked him. How long can you do this?

"Just watch me. Pierre Trudeau," he said, and laughed, or tried to, but it turned into a yelp that startled us both. He closed his eyes. He trembled. And wept.

~

"They've forgotten you," I told the boy. "That's all right, they've forgotten you." But I knew they did not forget people. Not these people. They had an exact plan in mind. Never mind the freeloaders, they were old and there was still the argument publicly that they had earned some kind of respite, some kind of consideration, but these kids — there was no way. In that little room there was one window, but it was covered. I couldn't reach it to let in some light. Probably there was no light to let in. Probably it opened into another room, or a blank wall somewhere, the wall white brick, painted yearly, or some kind of metal, sandblasted once a year. There are certain standards for buildings. Where they came from you never know. You depend on the window being there. You can't depend on it being useful.

The boy held the handle of my knife, absent-mindedly, and his wound held the blade, as if it were all natural. Do these hospital characters think they are above the law? There must be one rule that founds our belief.

"I will keep the knife in. They will be here soon."

"No. Take it out."

"I am the one stabbed. I am not the one stabbing. They'll be here soon."

"What is your name?" I asked him, leaning down to his ear, whispering. We were in a hospital. We had all the gear and the body is simple.

He asked me which one, he said he had many names and when he was a child . . . I removed his hand from the knife. I wheeled the boy and my knife out of the room. Everything in the hospital was at my disposal. There were empty beds and empty rooms and empty hallways and the wheels and my footsteps had authority there in the silence. Questions were not asked.

~

I'm not made of money, so I can't explain this taking cabs everywhere. Why not take the subway? Why not take a bus? I could even walk, as I had until this morning, until stabbing the boy.

I planned on walking, but found myself in a taxi. Shut up, I told the driver. I'm sorry. I am private.

The birds that strut around don't know the world has changed. Their poor, ridiculous brains miss the essentials. Every time the cab stopped, a bird was there pecking at nothing, or walking in jerky movements like an unbalanced toy. Sometimes in the morning you see them cooing, burying their hard beaks briefly in each other's feathers.

Every block I told myself it's time to get out and walk, but stayed in the taxi, looking through its glass. People bumped into one another on the street as we stopped, again and again, at lights. Bareheaded women tried to look straight ahead. Children yelped and laughed on their way home. And everywhere, people exchanging objects, trying to be civil.

It Cools Down

THE MAN WAVED TO HIS TWIN boys as they drove away with their mother in that polite old station wagon. I could only see the sweaty, rumpled back of him, with the hair on his neck damp and dark. But I said to myself, Jesus, this one's going to go on about everything.

He shook his coat out and folded it again over his left arm, then turned to walk toward the school as the sun hung low in the sky. He was startled to see me there behind him, and briefly on his lined face was the ghost of a frown, then a sudden smile.

"Hey," he said through his white teeth. "Is this where the meeting is?"

"Sure," I said. "We just got all the chairs arranged. Just stepped out for a smoke."

I knew he thought it was a filthy habit. Everybody did. So did I. But he just stretched his hand out and told me his name, Bob Rush. I told him mine: Larry.

"Well, good to meet you."

"Yeah, you too, Larry. Look, is this air-conditioned? Will it be cool in there?"

"It's a pretty old school," I said. He sounded like a salesman.

"Yeah. No luck huh, Larry? No air-conditioning?"

"No," I said. I knew he must be a salesman, the way he kept saying my name.

"Look, I just moved here, Larry, just last month. Is this normal? I mean, Jesus, it cools down, doesn't it?"

I knew it. Cripes. About the weather, no less.

"It cools down, Bob. It's an odd year."

"Yeah, it's odd all over, I guess."

I didn't know what he meant, and so I asked him. Behind him, on the other side of the street, a kid stopped his bike to pick up something he'd seen in the grass. He held it up to his face. The poor kid had glasses an inch thick. He put whatever it was in his pocket and rode on as fast as he could.

"I mean the weather," Bob said. "It's hotter than hell here, then there's all that flooding in the east."

"I'm just worried about what's coming when this is over," I said, looking at the sky. I wanted to scare him. Maybe we get tornadoes here, that kind of thing. But he was calm and looked at me, just waiting for an explanation. I lit another cigarette.

His wife had just driven off. She was leaving — otherwise, why would he be at the meeting? — and here he was, chatting me up like a salesman.

What about the anger? What about walking two steps toward the dust that hung behind the gone car and shaking your fist? But then the kids. The kids were the point of it, after all. It had to be right for the boys.

If it were me?

There was nothing to do but your mind goes on. I could picture it all. The real story was in the car. A road trip gets things moving. Bob was stuck with us. His twin sons looking back at him through the bright air, with their young faces bumped up against the glass, would they be consoled during the trip ahead?

Would they even need consoling? And this wife, with her solid, straight course of action, with her defiant turn out of the parking lot and her every direction sustained by active physical pressure on the car, either fingers and hands turning the wheel or a foot holding steady on the pedal, would she set the twins down somewhere as it got dark? Would her two boys eat, confused but open to this new adventure? It wasn't forever; nothing, so far, had been forever. Everything, so far, had ended up all right.

Meanwhile, Bob was stuck with us. It's the right way to do things, these days. The women have their support groups, why not us, Bob? Why not us indeed, Larry? Your wife tells you to go and get your support — for you and the kids you all need to do things right — you the father, and she the mother.

But would the mother sit outside the tiny roadside restaurant and smoke a cigarette calling on as much as she could see in the night sky to justify whatever it was she thought she was doing?

So here was Bob, talking to me about the weather. The sun does all it can, Bob. The meeting is about to start, Bob. Welcome to our community, Bob. This is what happens here.

"Well," he said. "Isn't that something? Would you look at that?"

I followed the line of his sight. I looked over to where he was looking. It was a pretty big deal. His old station wagon sat in a little driveway four doors down from the schoolyard.

The air seemed to hold the ghosts of the sounds of car doors closing. It was Penny's place. She just moved there, but everybody knows Penny.

"Are you going to do anything?"

"What could I do, Larry?"

"Some people do things, Bob."

"What kinds of things?"

I shrugged. Listen, Bob, I thought, I am the wrong guy to ask. I didn't do anything. My wife left long ago and though I had one son, not two of the same, not twins, I did nothing. It's a very small town and I should have known where she'd go. I knew where she'd gone. I've seen it many times. Penny's. Penny is a big help. It's a safe place.

He took the doorknob in his hand and turned. I usually struggle a bit with this door, but he opened it easy. I'm older than he is and also I have an undiagnosed disease I call arthritis. Maybe it is, or maybe it isn't, but when I use that name people know what I mean.

The meeting was about to get underway. Gord and Jamie introduced themselves, as they usually did, then I introduced Bob and myself, though I needed no introduction. It was how things went in these meetings; we all introduced ourselves every time.

Gord was wearing a button-up shirt and his sleeves were not rolled up. Jamie had on an old T-shirt with dark stains of sweat all over it. The shirt said something about a 10 K Fun Run, but Jamie looked like he'd never run a day in his life. He was a solid shape with a huge hard belly, thick all over with his big arms and shoulders solid muscle. Hair jumped out from the neck hole of his shirt.

The interior darkness was a switch from the sun outside and the hardwood floor was a sickly colour. There were six empty chairs in the middle of the gym. I sat down but Bob walked back to the exit after putting his jacket on the chair beside me.

We all waited for him. This wasn't usually done. The meeting had begun. So we watched him as he opened the fire exits, then came and sat back down. He looked at us all and smiled.

"Sorry," he said. "But it's so hot in here."

Jamie nodded and so did Gord.

"It doesn't help," I said. "That's the only thing."

"Maybe a breeze will get through here."

"There's no wind," I said.

"It doesn't hurt," Bob said. "Now how does this work?"

"He's right, Larry, it doesn't hurt. Sometimes there's a breeze." Gord shuffled some papers that he held on his lap. He squinted at me as he spoke. We heard a car drive slowly on gravel outside, the sound of a child's surprised and happy scream followed by laughter. And somewhere, just at the range of my hearing, a lawnmower stopped and another expectant layer of silence was added.

"No, I guess it doesn't," I said.

Jamie rubbed his eyes and said, "It works like this."

Bob watched Jamie, who took a while to speak anyway, but especially when someone was new. He wanted to remember exactly how it had been explained to him.

"We introduce ourselves?" Bob asked, turning in his chair from Jamie to me. His short neck was almost useless; he swivelled his whole upper body from his hips.

"Well, yes," Jamie said, and Bob swivelled back to him.

"But we've already done that, Bob," I said, just to see the poor man turn toward me again. But he stood up and pulled the chair back, away from the group, then sat down on it again where he could see us all just by turning his head a few degrees.

"He means formally," Jamie said.

"Sure I do," Bob said. "I mean formally, like in AA."

"There is no formality here," I said.

"Maybe Bob would like the formality," Jamie said to me, and then to Gord: "We used to be more formal."

"I don't know," I said. Things weren't going the way I expected. We hadn't had to go through these motions for quite some time. We just talk. We know who we are.

"Especially in a small town, I think, Larry," Gord said. "The formality may help us seem a bit more like strangers or at least give us the impression that we have some kind of anonymity."

Bob nodded.

"We don't, of course," Gord said, and rubbed the end of his nose with the back of one hand.

"I think it would help me," Bob said finally.

"Then let's go ahead, Bob," I said. "Let's start with you."

Bob stood up and walked back and forth in a short line in front of us. He looked at the floor and paced, then he went to his chair, put his hands on its back, and looked at all three of us in turn.

"Somebody else had better go first," he said. "This just happened to me. Everything's just happened. I haven't been to a meeting like this before. I was just dropped here and I met Larry outside while they drove off."

Bob was sweating. He stopped talking and stared at me. Jamie and Gord were looking at me too. I knew this would happen. I knew it would and now they wanted me to clear things up, they wanted to hear what I knew. I nodded and tried to smile.

"I don't need to introduce myself," I said. "Why don't you go first, Gord?"

Gord looked at the papers in his lap. He cleared his throat.

"Okay, my name is Gord," he said, then cleared his throat again. "I used to be called Gordie."

"Right," I said. "Then you went to Gordon, which you liked. Now it's just Gord, which you're unsure about but it will have to do."

"Jesus. Would you just let him speak?" Jamie said.

I didn't say anything. I let him go on. Of course it's the right thing to do but I'd heard it again and again, formally and informally. Now what?

I stood up and walked to the door. There were two of us standing now, Bob and me. Bob was holding the back of his chair, sometimes gesturing with his hands or standing straight as if stretching, but he never moved from behind his chair.

I stood over by the northeast door. It was just as hot in the shade of the interior as in the light let into the gym by the open door. But there was a breeze, just like they said. I couldn't help it. I lit a cigarette. I need something to do with my hands. Nobody would say anything. It wasn't that bad.

I heard the ice-cream boy riding his ice-cream cycle on the other end of town. I imagined screen doors on rusty hinges slamming, and children running with money in their hands. A Fudgecicle. Sitting on the step, with my arm tired from throwing the ball, my son beside me who could catch and throw all night.

I went back to Jamie and Gord and Bob, just about the time Gord finished his little introduction. Bob, in his loosened tie and shirt wet from sweat, walked the two steps over and pulled Gord from his chair to give him a hug. Jamie looked a little uncomfortable. He stood and squeezed Gord's arm.

Everybody sat down again, except for Bob and me.

"I don't know if I completely understand," Bob said. "I moved here two weeks ago with my family. My wife had twins. I mean she gave birth to them eight years ago. We have twins. Their names are Art and Zach. Those were not my choices but I like them. They're not as plain as Bob. I always wanted for my kids names that were not as common as Bob. I couldn't think of names on my own but Debbie did and I like them now. I wanted maybe Zeus or Thor, that kind of name. That kind of odd name.

"Two weeks ago we moved to this town. No offence, but I didn't want to. I mean, it's a good place to raise kids, and I was happy for them, and I'm glad they're here.

"But it's just so far outside my realm of experience, I didn't know anything about it."

Bob was telling a story. This was not an introduction. I was pacing up and down the floor.

"They're not that far, Bob," I finally said, interrupting him. Jamie looked at me and stood up. He was getting annoyed. Gord looked as if he pitied me, just like he always does. "I'm just saying," I said. "They're right down the street.

They're at Penny's place, they're just down the fucking street! They're right there!"

Jamie stood like he always did; he seemed to get closer without ever moving. I calmed down. I walked to the door again. I lit a cigarette and listened to Bob's voice.

Bob's story went like this: He had two kids. Twins, as I said. They were boys and he loved them. He suspected from the beginning they weren't his sons.

The usual reasons would have been mathematical, but Bob didn't think of anything like that. He'd been on the road, sure, selling construction equipment. He'd been in different cities on some nights and he'd been out late all the time.

But what made him think they weren't his was the subtle change in his wife, Debbie. She'd been happy the last few months before the pregnancy. She'd taken to kissing him the moment he came in the door from a trip. She'd drag him everywhere when he wasn't on the road.

One Saturday morning he'd been lying in bed, dozing, and she took a phone call in another room. The long and the short of it is, she took that phone call and something changed. It happens when you're not paying attention so that in retrospect it seems sudden — a barely heard voice, a new habit clung to out of love, a surprised physicality — she's your wife but you are a stand-in for her new lover. She's been tender but only because it overflows. And one morning, she is crushed by a phone call while Bob is half-asleep. Then after the twins were born, she was happy again and it happened suddenly.

One day, it was tax day, he was getting more and more frustrated, adding the numbers. I don't know what happened next, but fair enough. I got tired of listening. The sun was going down outside. The long sky was stretching pink, the colour of candy.

The gist of poor Bob's story was his wife had moved them to this little town, this minor spot where I've lived my whole life. She wanted, now, after this long, to be near the kids' father. Bob was trying to do the right thing.

I stood there by the door while the world outside changed colour. Bugs were killed in zappers. Other bugs whined nearby.

Now Bob was here with us. Bob was trying to do the right thing. It's unnatural, it's not right. Like ill-fitting clothes. Like a child swimming in his father's fucking jacket. Where has the man gone?

"As long as it's not my fault," I heard Bob say.

"Nobody would blame you," Gord said.

"You guys are a big help," Bob said, trying to smile.

But no, they are not. There is a tremendous lack of understanding here. Blame has got nothing to do with it. We are already blamed. We cannot get around it.

My own mother blamed me for everything when Lena left. I went over it in my mind. No, I said, I did nothing wrong. She said I could have done more.

It does not change one fucking thing, thank you.

She apologized later, when we drove by Penny's. Lena was somewhere inside. My boy Jasper sat on the stoop.

It never rains in this town. I turned the wipers on accidentally. Don't smile. Don't cry. I wanted to be a good example in my mother's car, so I tried to signal as I turned away from my boy on the stoop. The wipers waved. I honked, though I'm sure it seemed like a mistake.

I lived two blocks from Penny. Where was my wife?

My mother said she was sorry, she said she saw how much it hurt me. Doesn't change a thing, I know, but I listened. I said nothing because I knew it would lead to more listening. I was tired of listening. To be honest, I thought of horrible crimes I had seen on TV. I could picture myself cleaning my gun, looking out to the street through a wrecked door.

I held it in the best I could. Now, with Bob and Gord and Jamie supporting each other behind me, the air was not getting cooler but the darkness was there. It was another night of still, hot, air. The windows were all open everywhere, I knew. Television lights were on everywhere, porch lights, dim basement lights, but it was to be avoided; everyone is afraid of the heat even a small bulb will give. It is one more absurdity.

There was a light on upstairs at Penny's and it was in my mind but I heard twin voices praying. These voices were clean. The wet hair was parted in the middle. They'd found gifts in their little beds of new pajamas, just for boys who were leaving their father. This was the charity you might find beside the fucking penny tray at the Lucky Dollar.

Bob was talking and Gord and Jamie just listened.

"I can't take this," I said.

They had all forgotten I was there. Jamie looked at Bob and waited for him to continue.

"Something's got to be done," I said. I walked around the gym and closed all three fire exits. "All this does is let the bugs in."

I went over and stood in front of Bob.

"Something's got to be done, Bob. I'm going now," I said, shaking his hand. "Good to meet you. Good luck. You guys stay here all night. You talk the fucking thing out, Bob."

"Larry, sit down," Jamie said, but I couldn't.

~

Standing in front of Penny's, I couldn't think of what to say. She had no doorbell. I banged on the door. It was like balsa wood. It was like an airplane kit. The driveway was empty and a light switched out upstairs.

"The sun's been down for an hour," Bob said. I turned and saw his waiting face. I thought I heard a sound behind the thin door — a child, or children, padding down the stairs for a drink of water after a nightmare — as Bob put his hand on my shoulder and walked me out to the street. "I can't believe this place," he said. "Does it ever get cooler?"

He was waiting for some kind of explanation from me, some kind of defense of what went on here. But I was through talking. There was no light whatsoever on that street. There were no distinct shapes and I was not talking. I was tired of talking. Enough talking, Bob, I wanted to say, but I was tired of talking. There was no more.

Everything Is Loud

RAY HELD THE EDGE OF THE table to lower himself into the chair. He knew he'd become old slowly, as everyone did, but sometimes, like now, he felt he'd taken one huge leap away from his youth. He was aware of how he must look to the boy at the counter.

His hands shook when he didn't concentrate. His ears were full of hair. He had to carry a hanky to wipe the corners of his mouth because his bottom lip hung down. He still smiled, but it was an awkward thing. He still had a good smile — better than ever, actually, since his false teeth were beautiful and straight. But he had to cough sometimes as the excess saliva was flushed into his mouth by his bottom lip tightening in the smile. It was like when he was a child and had to swallow, for some reason, a viscous and dirty medicine that numbed his tongue and made him cringe at the same time.

The horrible medicine was always followed by the comfort of heat spreading from the ugly taste in his mouth down to the ache in his chest. He'd made his children drink the same stuff, and it worked, though one of them was dead, he remembered, but not from a chest cold. Now, after a smile and the indignity of a little dribble from the corner of his mouth, or a tiny and, he hoped, inaudible and otherwise unnoticeable slurp, he felt no comfort, though the medicinal taste remained. He paused and brought the hanky up to his mouth just in case. He smiled again, but okay — nothing happened.

Glancing down as he stuffed the hanky into his right pocket, he saw some newspaper on the floor. It was some kind of flyer and he had to adjust again. He leaned on his left hand, still on the table, and pulled his cane from where he'd tucked it under his right arm. Now he had to be very careful

He'd seen this happen before — you believe you're on solid ground, but you're not. You put your weight on it and it's gone. What was the flyer for anyway? With the rubber tip of his cane he pulled it out into the aisle a bit, out of the way of his foot. What were they selling? He couldn't tell, but he could see next year's date in huge numbers written boldly and knew he wouldn't have to pay until then. Until sometime in the hypothetical future which he didn't know he wanted to believe in.

Finally seated, he sighed and dabbed the left corner of his mouth. He laughed about the hypothetical future. It had all been a theory, of course — no promises — but he'd believed in it as a certainty, and did his eighty-second birthday prove he'd been right to let it slide, to believe in his future without doubt, to believe it was his right?

His wife was in the casket in the other room. Nancy. His wife's name was Nancy. He was not so old that he'd forgotten her. What he remembered and what he forgot was always surprising to him.

But the sun shone in and warmed his hand as it lay on the table. You can still take pleasure in simple things. Like when he'd come in out of the rain in his youth, when he'd changed from his wet clothes into dry and clean in the hotel room. That was the simplest thing he'd ever loved and he'd tried, sometimes, to recreate it in the summer, when he'd had money and no need to work in the rain. But you couldn't. You needed to suffer in the cold rain to appreciate the dry wool socks and the heater in the truck as you drove to get dinner.

But it was his wife he was thinking of. Nancy. She was in the next room, in a casket, and even then, over forty years ago, he'd known he would live and this was his burden to bear. Not a burden, really, but there was some difficulty. He would have wished the burden on Nancy, he would have wished her still alive. He did.

Oh, had everyone he ever remembered really died? It seemed impossible with the world going on around him, and his head warmed by his thick toque. The woman behind the counter seemed familiar.

He remembered a vacation, early in the summer; before she'd drowned, his daughter wouldn't go with him to the races in the town by the lake. They'd driven up to the race track a little late, because it had been a bad day for Nancy. The drag races had already started.

"Are you afraid?" his daughter had said, sitting straight on the seat beside him.

"There's nothing to be afraid of," he said, and smiled at her.

"No."

"They're loud, that's all," he told her. "Not dangerous."

"I know, but I don't want to go," she told him, and it was true. He could see it in her hazel eyes that just got wider and waited for his response. They never took their seatbelts off, and when they pulled out of the parking lot he saw his daughter looking fragile and neat after all day at the beach. He was glad he'd looked into her eyes.

"I don't know why everything has to be so loud, anyway," he told her, and she smiled.

He set his coffee down and wiped his chin. This child at the other end of the doughnut shop was blushing. The two boys with her were quiet, but she was loud.

"But why do you think I'm pretty?" she asked, and if they did answer it was too quiet for Ray to hear.

Here was a problem that could not be solved.

When Nancy, his first wife, was in the other room in her casket, he was accosted by all sorts of people. He remembered only a few of them but one in particular stood out, even now, in this Tim Horton's.

He didn't know what the purpose of the memory was. He was here to celebrate finalizing his will, getting all his affairs in order, which had not been easy. Seldom had he felt especially proud of his life and, in fact, given the way his ruminations had become increasingly out of his control, he had not felt a thing that could be clearly recognized as pride for a long time, and today he wanted to enjoy it.

But his wife, Nancy, kept lying, still, of course, in a casket in the other room, while her estranged friend accosted him, where responsible people stood by the coffee urns set on a long collapsible table against the windowless wall painted some kind of peach, which he wasn't sure was faded, or was it supposed to be that dull and flat, and someone's idea of comforting? And while he received the words of these well-meaning, responsible people, including one cousin who lived in the same city but was a stranger, except to Nancy and Nancy's pastor, who did his best not to make Ray feel guilty for not attending church, ever, he marvelled at the way vague things about tragedy came out of their mouths and he couldn't get his own ideas of tragedy out of his mind. Had his wife's life, had Nancy's life, been a tragedy or was his life the tragedy? If everyone's life were tragedy, if we all should just remain seated and weep at the end of each and every person's inevitable failure to live forever, then the word, and the world, lost all meaning.

Of course, he couldn't believe his life was the tragedy just because he was in his early forties and alone. He had enough money by then and he felt he could go on — no disrespect to Nancy. In fact, the tragedy was that she could not go on. Her life had been truncated, not by the full stop for which any sane person may hope, but by an ellipsis, as the disease worked slowly. It was efficient, mind you, it was not sloppy; it worked slowly and inexorably; it had time to spare and it shut each system off so smoothly — if it had been some kind of craftsman, if he could personify it in any way, he wouldn't know whether to respect its attention to detail and deliberate work or hate it for milking it, for piling on the billable hours when the end result required nothing so methodical — and by the time she died there was so little left for the disease to kill.

One night they'd spoken about Madge, this friend who accosted him now, in his memory, as she had accosted him that day in the refreshment room at the viewing, and both he and Nancy had tried to think of other, more positive things. The love Madge had for their daughter who drowned — but they couldn't get past her blaming Nancy. His wife was in the next room and still. She looked uncorrected, unreal, smooth and plastic, though she was not. He'd known by dressing her for the last time. This was her body, it was not plastic, but there is no way they could correct what the disease had done, no way to add weight, nothing to awaken.

Madge stared at him stupidly, her eyes big in the huge upside-down plastic frames that certain women of the era favoured, and Ray became angry, and for a moment forgot that he was still firmly anchored in the present, simply waiting a moment for his coffee to cool, and for the woman to bring him his slice of pie. He was angry for something so simple and stupid: why was it that he couldn't enjoy a memory without imposing the views of the present upon it? Not that he was actually enjoying it, if he were honest with himself — the woman was infuriating — but was it fair to focus some of his anger on the stylistic choice she'd made when most women around her made the same choice? Were the stupid-looking glasses just a distraction or were they part of the problem? Even at the time he may have felt that there was something wrong, something even despicable, perhaps, about a person who chose, continually, the path of least resistance, especially in terms of aesthetics, where taste was all that mattered and nothing was really at stake. So maybe it was part of what had made him angry back then, over forty years ago, though he appreciated the fact that she didn't say "It's such a tragedy."

If she had said "It's such a tragedy," as so many did, he would have been spun one more time into considering the tragic, and he always thought of tragedy as requiring a hero, and then who was the hero? Of course, Nancy had fulfilled partially the role of the modern tragic hero at the end of her life — and this is what brought tears to his eyes — when her eyes showed too clearly and easily the quick movement that used to belong to her body. This is not me, her eyes seemed to say, but without pity, without fear. He knew that. At least he knew. She didn't have to worry, but with all that time to sit and wait, he was afraid there was nothing else for her to do.

And that was fine, for despite the Hollywood movies, despite the stoic hero dying on the beach or in the water — despite movies ruining life, she was a hero. Anyway, who else could be?

He didn't believe in the noble person with the tragic flaw. And this woman, Madge, accosting him now . . . Of all the things that bothered him about aging, it wasn't the blue-spotted skin on the back of his hands, or the way his thick nails always looked yellow and already like the nails of a cadaver — he turned his hand over now in the sunlight and tried to see its palm as it had been, years ago, when he was a child, but how could he? He sputtered out a small laugh, then picked up the white china mug by its handle, amazed in this context that his fingers could commit to such delicate movements as this and he brought the cup to his mouth for a sip of coffee. Of course what would happen in even two months was too much to say — he remembered his grandmother needing two hands to hold a tiny cup of tea to her lips and everything wobbled. He gently lowered his mug to the table as he remembered her taking such care and trembling so much.

But it was his wife, Nancy, he was thinking of, and he remembered that he was sorry he was aging, though how regret entered into it he wasn't quite sure. He simply wished that he wasn't forgetting what he hated about the woman, Madge, or was hate too strong a word? But regret? What to regret about aging — that he was doing it, that he was alive? He couldn't regret his life, but there was something, and he remembered what it was: Why had he taken Nancy to Vancouver at the end, and — that's it! He hated Madge because she'd blamed Nancy, and he slammed his fist on the table. It shocked him, and he felt his eyes widen and he thought he might cry.

"Dammit! Where is it?" he said, loudly, and surprised himself with another fist on the table. He couldn't find the one thing he wanted to think of and stick to it. Then in his anger he might start to cry because the goddam movements of his own body startled him. He tried now to regain his composure. He put his elbows on the table and covered his eyes with his hands. What is the world going to think of him?

"Sorry about that," the young woman from the counter said, as she set a slice of chocolate pie on his table. "I forgot about your pie."

"It's okay," he said, looking up at her. "I wasn't upset about that."

"It's okay," she told him, and smiled, and he could see it was true even if he was an angry old man waiting angrily for some pie and slamming his fist on the table like some kind of baby. He saw that it was okay to her. She had other things on her mind, her own things, and he bet she shuffled through them like they were a stack of colour-coded index cards and, no matter what, the right image came to her mind, and that's why she was sure, and that's why she could be kind. He imagined what he must seem like to her and his eyes felt large and open. Everything was right out in the open.

But when he said no, and shook his head, he was sure she thought the gesture was just the normal shaking of a palsied old man. She went back to the counter and he looked for some of the other young people, afraid they were angry at him for causing such a scene, and one of the boys was gone, and the girl was less happy, and not blushing. He could tell the boy she liked was gone. It was a shame the boy still there didn't see it.

Still, it was anger he was after and he couldn't remember why. Maybe it was anger at himself — he'd come here to celebrate, to get himself a small treat, and he'd even said that to the boy at the counter while the girl pouring his coffee greeted him.

"Hi young fella," she'd said. "How's it going today?"

That's what had gotten him smiling, needing to wipe his mouth. And he'd seen the four digits on her name tag and remembered she was Anna. Why don't we all wear name tags? The world is so civilized with names.

"Fine," he said, and felt himself blush a little. "What about you?"

"Only an hour left till my shift is over," she told him.

Then the boy about to take his money said, "Is that all?"

"No. Today I'd like a slice of chocolate pie," he said, and continued, more for the girl, who was always there when he came in, than for this new boy, who he didn't know. "You see, I did something really good today."

But the boy was already ringing it up and just told him the cost, and the girl was already in the back, and Ray watched the swinging doors to the kitchen and saw one of the bakers laugh at something he couldn't see or hear, and now, remembering that, he couldn't remember what had been so good. He knew it had to do with completing his will, with making all the arrangements, and he knew his will gave the money to someone, but was this anger he wanted to feel because of that?

He knew his daughter's death wasn't Nancy's fault, but he knew others disagreed. He could see it now: that woman Madge, with her fish eyes and stunned look, saying she was sorry. What for? For the way she'd treated them both after that summer. But everyone had treated them that way, even years later.

"Don't!" he heard someone hiss, then looked up to see the young girl blushing, and the boy walking out the door beside her, slowly and shaking, with a thin line of spittle hanging from his open mouth.

Ray took his hanky from his pocket and wiped the corners of his mouth, then replaced it. The parking lot outside was darkening and he stared at the doors, just forgetting something else, and kind of shocked by the cold air that had come in when the kids left. He picked up his fork and cut into the pie.

The young girl was suddenly beside him and he looked up but he couldn't talk because his mouth was full.

"Sorry about that," she said.

She was waiting for him to speak, but he couldn't. He looked into her eyes and lowered his fork to the plate, then pointed at his mouth. She waited and he tried not to think of how he must look. He lowered his eyes and finally swallowed.

He felt her hand on his shoulder and without thinking he reached up and covered it with his. She didn't pull away and he smiled.

"No," he said. "Don't worry about it."

And the wrist, as he removed his hand and did his best to smile cleanly, reminded him, of course, of his wife's wrist. Nancy, who was in the next room. When she'd died she'd been the size of a child herself, and it wasn't the same beach they'd looked at, but still. They sat on the balcony there in Vancouver and watched the sun set over English Bay, but she'd been stuck in her body, and what if she hadn't wanted to be held? He'd been selfish.

And what if she hadn't wanted to see water?

But had he been angry? That girl and the boy she didn't like were gone, and the girl from behind the counter sat down across from him. Anna. She sometimes did that. Sometimes she walked him home and, once — he could remember with such clarity the act itself, the delicate memory, nimble and young, held in whatever calloused part of himself could still hold such a thing — they had stopped on the bench outside his building before going up. The world smelled of freshly cut grass and it was still early enough in the spring that they enjoyed the sunshine without removing their coats, and her young boy ran from the school bus. Or somewhere, he ran from somewhere — this part was not coming back to him but never mind because the boy ran with his shoes that lit while he ran and he jumped one jump into Ray's lap. And it must have been because he'd just run from out of the sunlight toward the dark shade of the building, but the boy hugged him tightly to his face like he'd known him his whole life and no one corrected him. Ray could picture the boy's face, with its fierce smile, as his little arms squeezed him with all their strength. Then, without thinking, he was standing, and he didn't go into the building and up to his room, but walked with mother and son to someplace in the fresh air, he didn't know where, and the boy talked the whole way, like boys do, and it was nothing to remember everything.

Leave Her Alone

A MAN WALKS INTO A BANK, rubbing his throat. He is dressed in a groovy coat and humming stuff into the air. What a gas! He doesn't unwind his scarf, man, 'cause that's working too.

What do you do? he thinks to the head of the lady in front of him. It's a long line. He thinks questions of each of them. He thinks things like How do you do? What do you do? and Why do you do? which is just a question his old English teacher kept hammering home. Ha! Why indeed.

But the woman in front of him he really did just wonder what. What do you do? Never mind she was a kind of maid he bet. Not a maid but maybe a nanny. He met a nanny once and the nanny was about that height, which is to say, there is a height for a nanny in this poor man's mind.

Anyway, the man walks into a bank and finds himself behind the nanny who he thinks is a nanny due to her height, which he estimates by looking from her to the doorway where the measuring stick for robbers is. Because he's worked for a long time in precise measurements, he tries to calibrate the measuring stick beside the door with the world around it. He is, himself, six feet and two inches, but he had never measured from his top point to his eyes, though he estimates, correctly, the distance is 4 ½ inches. That would mean he should be looking at 5' 9 ½" on the ruler (and he is).

But the man is feeling so good he's a little sloppy on the swivel of his head. His head bobs a little, man, in between his laser-like straight-edge eye measurements and the air above the back of the nanny's head. And that's because of the song in his car, the song singing: Well, when will I be back home?

Soon, man, soon. He will be back home soon. There is just this stop at the bank before the trip. The song is more mournful than the man's own celebratory mood. He's going home free and clear, with no bones to pick, no scores to settle, no money to beg, no bills of any kind. Just love there, man. Just love.

Why don't some of these beautiful creatures around him look to him with questions? Why doesn't the nanny, for instance, turn around and open up her smile? But she can't be the nanny, though she is so similar — the eyes in his swivelling head measured her too tall. She is too tall to be that nanny, but never mind she is a nanny here — they are all people in his world, man, and he loves them all.

They have the weight of the world on their shoulders. He sees it, and he knows it's because they are hanging on to their precious egos, and he almost slipped, in fact, when he thought of the nanny ahead of him, the perfectly dressed little woman who reminded him of a nanny he'd dated long ago. Let's be honest: he was obsessed. She gave him a new world and he believed in all of it, man. But he lost himself. He was gone.

It still caused a little pop in his head. It still opened a little space in that hollow cage of signs. He had lost himself, but not the right way. The right way was love, man, not desire. It had taken so long for him to learn, but that's okay. This is no race. And then this small woman in the bank line almost triggered a relapse. He wanted briefly, before the desire could form into words, that nanny to be his nanny. He knew he could love her now.

He felt like he hadn't eaten for a long time, a long long time. Something odd was on the inside of his sleeve. It was, oh yeah: he'd been to the blood bank. That's the kind of bank to be in. That's giving, man. Through his sleeve he pulled the little cotton ball from his skin, then shook his arm, trying to loosen the cotton, trying to drop it out of his sleeve and into his hand.

The others in the bank were all on the same journey. The old guy behind him wanted new stuff for his home. He had big gold rings on his knuckles. He smelled the baby smell of old men who'd done well, clean and powdered, with nothing but time. The sharp woman walking away from the other teller, jabbering into her tiny blue-and-grey earpiece — somewhere deep down she must want peace. We're all the same. We're all the same.

The man in the groovy coat wanted to hug them all to him and share this journey. He smiled. The nanny-sized woman in front of him was quick. There was a flurry of paper in and out of her worn purse, then she left the counter. He was still smiling as she turned around. She was not smiling, but she was very happy. Her eyes were alive, that's it; mischievous. That's okay, he thought. You play your tricks my little nanny. We can all love you without wanting anything back. He swivelled his head on a plane perfectly parallel to the floor and kept smiling at the nanny, then turned back to the teller.

His head bobbed a little as he set his gloves on the counter. He didn't look at the teller. I love this coat, man, I love this scarf, but I wish I could've been in the rat pack. I could be as cool as any of them, watching that little nanny walk away, going home, for no reason at all. He bobbed his head, then remembered where he was and smiled at the teller.

She looked at him with a closed mouth and handed him a slip of paper with precise handwriting in blue ink: *You have a gun. If I do whatever you want, I won't get hurt.*

But this is impossible. Is it possible? He looked behind himself. Has he misunderstood the way time works? Could he be going backwards? This is his world, isn't it? He felt his back pocket for his deposit slip. The teller shrieked. Everyone was on the ground. There were screams all around.

It's not that he hadn't paid attention. There was so much of greater importance with which to occupy his mind — the good feelings, man, the vibe that he was responsible for, the shit that made him live — it's true, there was so much of greater importance than the quick flight of papers between grabbing hands.

His hands had held each other sometimes, as he had watched the nanny he had dated, in the old days. Actually, she is the only woman he has loved. Actually, his grief at losing her was what eventually led to his discovery of this new way to live, which was, to be honest, working beautifully.

But when he and the nanny had been together, he seldom heard her words. Instead he might watch the thin hair on the top of her lip and wonder why on her it was lovely; why could he look right at it in wonder, why could he also stare for long moments at the birthmark on her shoulder blade and feel nothing but desire, despite the way this patch of skin the size and shape of a rodent was repulsive on its own? But he knew the answer was simple — she bore it, and it tasted like skin, like her all over again. He might stare at the thin wrists holding the bowl of latte to her lips and be amazed, as if she had engineered the entire fragile machine, only to reach the obvious conclusion that no, she was human, and had grown into her body as simply as he had. Still, that this delicate condition was not hers alone, that it was for us all, that bodies were being broken and destroyed every day, today, on this earth — it only made his love grow.

Of course it was unhealthy. He knew that now. Love doesn't need to know, man. Love doesn't look so closely; love doesn't need to explain. It just doesn't need. Keep your ego out of it, man. And playing it all back, looking at it all over, that's natural, but keep the word should out of it — you can't fix the past. There's no such thing as should.

He learned it all, but he couldn't forgive everything.

When he and she had spoken, now and then, her perfect smooth skin had swelled briefly below her brown eyes. It was a normal human response; it was an adjustment made on countless other faces. But because he had held the back of her neck in his hand, and because that hand had travelled down to her shoulder, to her cheek, down again to the tips of her fingers, and again, because he loved her, he wanted to take a thumb and touch that spot below her eye, and soothe it.

But it was gone so quickly, and meanwhile her voice continued its usual operations, her smile returned. Had that small look been sadness? Where did it go? Did he imagine it?

But he doesn't want to be fixed of this — he should have touched it. That sorrow should exist so physically, that it should be hidden, that its description should not love him . . . this was too much. He could not forgive her for this burden unshared. He would have worked, man, he would have worked.

~

But what does it matter, because the shrieking also brought bullets. It was a lucky shot, through the kneecap, from behind. Jesus Christ, man, shut that off. That hurts. I'm sorry. All sorts of things and through the pain he heard someone yell and oh no, they wanted him to put his hands somewhere and holy fuck it hurt so they were fluttering, man, they were fluttering; they shot up around him, even though it was only air, so if he were a rhino they would have just drugged him but no, that's what he thought, no, for a man just going home given some strange note, it's got to be bullets, it's got to . . .

~

The craziest thing: he was propped up in his bed, with his thin hospital gown on. Think positive, man, think positive. It was warm. He felt clean and there was his mother in a chair at the foot of his bed. He smiled at her, but then the craziest thing:

He was looking at six faces on a page. One cop held this in front of him, the other cop watched his eyes intently. He laughed. Where is my coat?

He kept laughing, looking into the cop's eyes, not looking at the paper at all.

We'll try later, the cop said, and his partner pulled the paper away.

It was just that funny, and then his mother was there, shoving a straw into his mouth. He obediently sucked the water and then started laughing again. He was choking and spit water onto his chest. Fuck, he said, turning red. Why did you do that?

His mother smiled sadly at the cops. It's the drugs, she said. It's not really him.

Hey, it's the drugs, he thought. That's true.

Okay okay, he said. It's just the drugs. I can do it now that I know. Show me the nannies please!

No, his mother said, and the policemen left through the door. Oh. It did feel good. Oh, they had left four bullets in a plastic bag on the table. Don't tell them, Mom. That's our evidence.

Wait a minute. It only felt like one. Whose bullets are those?

He smiled and asked his mother. Whose bullets are those?

They're yours honey, and this is your kneecap, she said, pulling a jar from her purse.

~

Wait wait wait, he said. Show me that again. It was a security tape being shown on the monitor above his bed. The nanny spoke briefly to the security guard at the bank door, then two seconds later the guard pulled his gun and fired four bullets.

Is all that necessary? he asked.

Concentrate on her face, the man with the remote said. Is that her?

I mean the bullets. I only felt one.

There were four.

I know that. I see those little pops from the gun, right? One, then a gap, then three more.

Four bullets.

Why?

The cop used the remote to pull the tape back to the nanny. Look, we've got a blow up of this one, he said.

You know who it is, the man said.

Yes.

Okay then.

He was still angry at his mother for giving the bullets to the cops. She sat at the foot of his bed still true, still smiling, still watching out for him. No, if she were watching out for him the morphine would be on its way right now. These cops wouldn't ask dumb questions.

We have the woman in question.

All the while, tape keeps rolling. It's from all the angles. He sees himself in his groovy coat falling to the ground. His hands are there in the air but they're moving. Stop it. He knows they should stop, he knows to lie still with his hands where they can see them, but one falls and stretches again to the ceiling, dropping a dark, bloodied swab of cotton into his mouth.

More bullets follow, of course, and he doesn't care about the nanny at all.

Let her go, he says, and his whole body hurts. Let her go, he says, feeling all his wounds. Then his mother's there with the nurse, looking ragged but trying to smile.

Don't let them take that tape, he whispers to her. Don't let them take the bullets or the tape.

His mother's smile fades and as he feels the morphine begin its work she puts her hand on his forehead. Shhh, you can keep your kneecap, she tells him. You should have been kind.

So Does the Body

There is nothing lush about his imagination. He sees one stick figure walking toward another, if he sees anything at all. There is no sun but the sky is lit. There is no remembrance of flesh, but the stick figure walks toward something. Or away, depending on the mood he's in.

Or one stick figure waits, with its legs crossed. Here, when this imagined thing waits, the green begins to grow. It's the first colour. The grass he may be sitting on (his gender insinuating itself easily, because he's still a man) is of course green, but this is less his imagination than a programmed default position.

Perhaps it doesn't matter how. Out of the normal syntax of things he has created a stick figure that assumes its own masculinity. Where the world and the stick figure meet, the world grows and so does the body. There is no need for a mouth, for eyes; the body knows its place in the world. It destroys every self that is not itself, automatically.

~

Later on, Ron sat at a table in an outdoor café. Someone came and took his cigarette from him, changed it to a cigar. Two men moved the table, then the man. He sat instead in a winged-back chair, thinking, just the same as he'd always thought. About the time he was younger and the things he had done wrong: Sure there was the beautiful girl he'd loved, but then he'd lost that love. And now he pictured her smiling in front of him, water flying as she shook her wet hair above him where he lay until he chased her back into the empty lake. He remembers it in black and white. He remembers it in colour. He shifts it around. It's changed again. He can't remember it anymore.

~

In the winter, once, Ron sat in a chair like this. It was long ago and he is finished thinking of it. So, where now?

Now he's in a white plastic chair outside the room of his motel. It's a small town in the interior of BC and the highway he faces seems particularly lonely today. It's October and the day is cool even though the sky is bright. It's before the sun has had a chance to touch everything, and he is just waking up.

His girlfriend, Jane, is gone into the city. It is not difficult to think of her as his girlfriend even though they have been together only two months. Not here, anyway, not where they have lived their whole time together. If they walked down a street in the city it would be hard. His wife lived there. Of course she is not his wife any longer. A lot of the thoughts he thinks need correction.

Jane goes to the city where they can't go together and gets meat and bread, gets wine that you can't get here. He sits outside their simple little door and waits for his brain to wake up. Then he'll take their laundry down to the hotel at the other end of town, the hotel where she'd stayed until all of this happened. Her company still paid, so what the hell? The laundry was cheaper there, but the room was smaller. Just a room. Here they had a kitchenette. Here they could cook. And now already they have their own jobs, he and Jane.

~

Somewhere on another planet his ex is describing him to her new lover. Not generously, but fairly; and only the parts that concern this new man.

"When you come home from work, you're not dirty," she tells him. And somewhere along the line, her new lover whispers words she can't hear.

"And I know you would never hit me."

Wait a minute. That was *his* new girlfriend. He had never hit anybody. That was *her* ex.

~

Sitting outside the motel, he waits for Jane, but she'll be gone all day. He doesn't think much about the story this is making. He doesn't think at all about: this really is the beginning. He's come into this life somehow. Here he is. Everything is better.

All the lines move quicker, because he's been in so many — bank lines, grocery store lines, traffic lines at bottlenecks of bridges. Lines outside bars don't move quicker, but he doesn't stand in them anymore.

But this is the beginning of his life. He'll learn it starts from here in a month or two. There is a doctor in town who takes on new patients. He'll go there for a yearly checkup. Nothing to worry about at all. There are pills for what will be discovered, and, actually, later he will feel perfect, because it was just a scare, nothing to worry about, and he and Jane will rent a home. It will be two years before his sudden awakenings end. They come without warning and he stares at the ceiling afraid that he's betrayed his ex-wife. In those spells, he cannot forgive himself for loving a new woman. He wakes up as fearful as if the doctor had found his life almost over, as if the determination was made that he should get his affairs in order.

He can't. His ex lives in the city and she is still the beneficiary and though no one is asking him to, he can't change that. He won't. But nobody is asking.

~

The story can start anywhere and most days it starts here, just before the laundry. He has brief spells of knowing the story begins years ago in the city. But here, in his daylight, by the side of this underused highway in October, Ron makes a decision to quit smoking. He imagines his deathbed and tries to feel Jane beside it, but cannot. His ex in the city is there, and he apologizes for everything, including killing himself the easy way. Now, it's hard to swallow. He doesn't want to regret out in the open, in this daylight. He stands and goes to pack up the dirty clothes.

And now, the man will go to do their laundry, perhaps picking up a story by Raymond Carver to read while the washing happens. He'll remember things in his own life that somehow resemble the things in the Carver story — not things like drinking on a couch on the lawn, urging a young couple to dance to a record played on the outdoor record player. Not things like that, but things generous to both of the women he loves — things like becoming friends with his ex-wife, things like all of them from everywhere having Christmas together somewhere warm while he tries his best to stay sober. That's something he could appreciate.

He will sit and read these old beautiful stories while his new girlfriend is in the city and their laundry tumbles in the machine. The smell of the softener when he holds her *Cats* shirt to his face will be the most tangible evidence of his new life. If he were more of a ladies' man he would know there are not enough scents in the world, not enough variety, for the smell to matter. But now all he knows is he likes this vanilla that Jane uses. He's been sick of his wife's floral scent for as long as he can remember.

~

He is only a stick figure, grown flesh by the motion of walking into the imagination, then being seated — he became human because he needed to rest. Work is implied, or fatigue. It's so easy to burden characters with weariness.

~

His flesh is becoming invisible again because his girlfriend, Jane, has just opened the door to his ex-wife's apartment. His ex-wife is about to say hello, but first she must take a lot in.

Jane is the first woman Ron has been with since they parted. She wants to like her, she really does, but must first take a look. Jane is a simple name. The woman named Jane has put on a little makeup, something unexpected. It looks unexpected, as well; a bit under-thought. Jane should be a thick woman, with a face brown and wrinkled by the weather, but she's not. Her lines are from laughing, but they're not sharp, they aren't cut in like the lines in the faces of women she sees holding stop signs by the side of the road, waving at traffic and smiling the best they can. She's a petite woman with hair she doesn't dye. She's a salt-and-pepper woman with a startled look in her eye.

"Hello," says Jane again.

"Hi," says Rhonda. "Come in."

~

This is where the story ends. Jane walks in and Rhonda lets her. Ron washes clothes and enjoys his time alone as only a new man can — without fear, without anticipation, sated. Nothing on TV matters to him but he watches it anyway.

~

There is a window downtown that shows the same game show Ron watches. Cheering and clapping you can't hear behind the glass. A short pudgy boy looks through the window at the prizes. Kids aren't allowed to make fun of his weight, though they do when they can, but they are allowed to make fun of the way he smells. He smells of urine. The teachers don't notice when the kids call him Cat, because his name is Tom, or so the teachers think.

It's short for cat-piss, really, because he smells like urine. He told one boy it's because his mother has so many cats, they piss all over his clothes. It's not true. The urine is his. He can't help it — he gets scared to move. People laugh at him when he moves. He tries to sit still at his desk until the next period. But he dribbles sometimes.

So these are the truths: the woman is his aunt, not his mother, and the piss is his own, not the cats'. But he has never had a better nickname. The boy Tom sits down on the sidewalk and watches the game show. The prizes bewilder. His nose runs a little and he uses his sleeve.

This is not where the boy imagines his own story starting, but it does. The aunt is trying her best but just wants to drink herself blind for a little while; she just wants to forget all the things she's done wrong. One of the things she's done wrong may turn out right. She's no good at raising Jane's boy, but Jane's all right now. She's much better.

She's sent a letter, about her life and the new man, Ron, who would never hit her. Tom hasn't met him yet, of course, but Jane knows they will love each other.

Who am I, anyway? the aunt thinks. I'm no better than Jane. Not at all. I'm the one who drinks, not her. Tom should be with her, that's true. With Jane and the new man who won't beat anyone.

~

Rhonda is just now consoling Jane, who's come to ask, to really ask, about Ron. She says I can't take the chance, I just can't. He never hit you, did he? And Rhonda answers, No, he never did, though he's got a temper. Jane looks up and her eyes are wide, her mouth is open. But who doesn't? Rhonda says, and Jane looks relieved. I want my boy back, she says.

Ron always wanted a son, he has always wanted a son but Rhonda doesn't say that. She looks at Jane and knows she feels anger, so she gets up and paces. She looks out the window at the same beach she has always stared at. Tiny people, of course. Tiny people too far away to be people. She knows they're people, of course. Everything is inevitable, she says out loud.

"What?" asks Jane.

"Why are you here? Get out. You can't just come and ask people questions. What kind of person — "

~

Ron never wanted a boy like this boy, wrecked already by something nobody could ever see. He wanted a son to pop into this world like an idea in the morning, fresh as hell, free all day. But Tom never wanted a father like Ron, who'd failed at everything until he met Jane. He didn't want to end up spending holidays with all these different characters. He wanted his fictional father to come home. He wanted his fictional mother to stop grieving his loss. He wanted his father to take shots on him then say you don't have to be goalie, you can skate if you want. He wanted his father to know that he smelled like his own urine and not hate him, which would never happen anyway.

Ron has finished his story so he looks up. The dryer is done just then. What luck, he thinks, and stretches. He doesn't know what he'll say to the boy when he meets him, but he's been thinking of it. He has no detail, no rich and gauzy scene set up for it. He won't tell him, look, I'm sober two years now, I'm the best I've ever been, I was not good for a while, but. He might say: But, look at it this way. I'm forty-five and I'm just learning how to be a father. I never thought I would. You got thirty-five years, mister, to catch up to me.

A Long Day Inside the Buildings

I ROLLED UP MY SLEEVES JUST to keep cool. The bus driver had his window open, too. What a day, he said, every time a regular stepped on. I'm done at two, he said, then I'm going down by the river with a cooler of beer.

It's the juxtaposition that does it, you know. This last winter had been cold. Cold. No respite. Cold and long. You walk away from the bus stop all those times and it seems like there will never be sunlight. You're either rich, with money to burn, or you've got to economize, and, out of guilt, or this desire to pinch pennies, you are rarely, if ever, comfortably warm.

Then, one day, warmth that seemed to happen as quickly as the flick of a switch. My mother always warned me not to stick my arm out of the bus. But I wanted to. That bus driver was taking a risk; he was letting everyone know. You can't always do that; a cooler of beer down by the river is fine but keep it to yourself, we've got a long day inside the buildings, ourselves.

The superintendent had explained the initiative in the new year. There is a dedicated phone line in the classroom. This is for one call; this is for when the head will answer a question. It was in reaction to all the clutter in the cellular and satellite communications. It was a return to the old days; a hard plastic phone on the wall, with a thick curled cord.

And today was the day. My children all had questions and we were to narrow them down today. Today we would ask our question. There had been no emergencies; we had not used the telephone in the room. But today the head would call us and we would ask our question.

~

They said keep the lines open and I knew what they meant. No ideology. Emergencies only, aside from the prescribed purpose. For example, a student of mine brought forward the notion, one day, of phantom pain.

"Where will you feel this pain?" the boy, Tommy, asked. "Will it be the exact dimensions of real pain? That is, will a size eleven foot still feel like a size eleven when it's actually gone?"

It was the first day of the year when we could open the windows, according to the rules, and according to the weather. I opened them all. Overnight, everything had changed, and here we were.

It was coming up to noon. It was approaching the deadline. This is exactly what I was getting paid for; this was facilitation.

"Okay, okay," I said. I was prepared to draw a chart.

~

The whole thing is lousy with implications. Think how easily you wave a hand in the air. If there is a ring on that hand, that can cut glass. Dangle your arm out the window of a truck, for instance, at the stoplight, in the summer time.

There is nothing ticking anymore, but we imagine a clock. We still hear the old ways of measuring time but . . . what about the heart? Generally, the heart beats. It generally beats like waves on a beach — organic, natural, it beats in this world, it sounds in our ear.

Think, Marshal, think! There is a way around this. Remember the rules. There are instances where a teacher, someone in your position, may override specific rules. Sure, sure, there are times, but these are also theoretical; they have to do with possibilities.

~

The problem was, I could not remember Mindy's problem, and to ask her again would be a disservice to her, as well. I had to remember they were all children, not just Tommy, the boy with the wrong foot.

How did this happen? How does this happen?

"Is it leprosy?" I asked, out loud, mistakenly. I had only been thinking.

"What?" the boy asked quietly. The room around him was quiet too. Only Mindy, with her added authority, being one of the authors of the two questions in question, was able to speak. She also asked quietly "What?"

"Never mind," I said. "I'm sorry. I was thinking of something else."

"No you weren't," said Mindy's friend. "You were not. You said is it leprosy. You meant his foot."

All the children looked at the boy's foot. Tommy himself was ready to faint, it seemed. He was a shade that resembles, if nothing else, leprosy, or what I associated with the disease. A kind of yellow. A distorted and deimagined take on the basic yellow — paler and more threatening — a kind of process implied.

"Jesus," Tommy said. "Is it leprosy?"

Now what? The children would tell their parents. They would tell their parents. Just what are you accusing this poor boy of? they would ask.

I knew there was no accusation. There could be no accusation where a disease was concerned, surely, but still — it was the kind of thing I could get in trouble for.

"Children," I said. "There is no such thing as leprosy. I was just thinking of the times we've learned about in history, remember. There were all these different things that happened. Even my mother used to use a phone like this one. It was making me think."

I was fading fast and I didn't know why I'd brought my mother into it. Many people had used these phones; there was no reason to implicate anyone.

"I remember that disease," Tommy said. I thought I saw him cheering up a little. I thought he changed back to his natural colour.

"Right," I said. "It was awful. But the one I was remembering was tuberculosis."

"That one's still around," Mindy said, sniffing.

"No it isn't," Tommy said. For the first time they looked directly at each other. There was a brief flash of communication between them. There was a spark of contempt in the eyes of each child. These children could still be primal.

"Not here, Tommy," Mindy said. "But out in the country, where they don't take care of themselves. My father told me."

We all knew who Mindy's father was. He was on the rules committee. He was one of the owners of the city. He was a minority owner of the province itself.

"Mindy," I said, trying to scold her. "You know that's not fair. Your father's opinions have no place here. He's just one person like all the rest of us."

"I'm sorry," she said, and turned on the tears again. Sue comforted her but I could tell she was on shaky ground with the rest of the class.

~

I went to the window and leaned out, briefly. Spring air filled my head. I couldn't get the bus driver out of my mind. A bit chilly to be down by the river, but I bet he was. I bet he was even there with a cooler of beer and his coat undone, smoking a cigarette and leaning his head back in the sun.

My father used to sit down by the river in the summer. He was the only smoker I knew and that was the smoking area. I would sit beside his lawn chair sometimes when I was Tommy's age. My father would lean his head back and look straight up into the sky. I leaned back too. Naked except for my swimming trunks, I was turning slowly brown. My eyes were always stunned by the sunny blue and I was often briefly blind. My father squinted all the time. I was sure he saw something I missed in those brief moments.

"Can't get a thing done, sitting here all day," he muttered once, just before I heard him snore.

Now, I saw a mother walking her daughter to the bus stop at the other end of the parking lot. The little girl was walking as fast as she could, but seemed to have a slight limp. One of her shoes fell off and she pulled her mother to a stop.

They both sat on the asphalt, facing each other, as the girl tied her shoe.

I needed to get to the problem. "Listen, Tommy," I said. "I understand your anxiety. I think we all do." I looked around the class, raising my eyebrows.

"Oh yes," they muttered, especially Mindy's contingent. "Of course," added Mindy herself, at which point her best friend, Sue, put a hand on her shoulder.

Mindy turned to Sue. There was such love in their eyes, they could not help but cry. So they did, falling into each other's arms.

Mindy said, wetly, through Sue's hair and into her shoulder (though we all heard; the classroom was that quiet), "Let Tommy go."

All the other children were filled, enlarged by Mindy's selflessness. I am supposed to facilitate, not adjudicate.

Tommy held his hands together tightly on his desk.

"My question is too theoretical," he said. "While the question itself is not hypothetical, it can be argued the possible use of its potential answer is largely hypothetical."

We all heard him, too, though he spoke, as always, softly. His hair was damp from sweat at the top of his forehead and he smiled weakly around at his classmates, finally letting his gaze rest on Mindy and Sue. They didn't look up, they just continued comforting and consoling each other.

What kind of chart can a man draw in such an instance? What kind of Department of Education Powerpoint presentation can teach these children when I can't? In the end of the story I accidentally cut one of Tommy's toes off. I only want to illustrate a point. I'm tired of the ritual obfuscation. I'm afraid.

I wanted everyone to see the boy's foot, and he took his pale shoe off to show me. It smelled like the hospital my mother died in. When he peeled his sticky sock off, I put my fingers around his ankle. Children, I said, Tommy's foot is diseased. It's awful, I said. This poor boy will have his foot amputated. The smell didn't bother me anymore and I held the bottom of his foot with my other hand. It was as rough as my crying father's cheek that day in the hospital. He tried to comfort me, too tightly. He said, let's go to the river. I couldn't leave my mother's room.

I held Tommy's foot and the five-minute bell went. We call it a bell, still, though many children have never heard a bell. I held the boy's foot and I said it would be cut off and he was to ask a simple question.

Mindy and the others saw the knife, and I said this is not hypothetical. I said, Children, this is the real question, while Mindy and her friend cried. Tommy squinted above his tight mouth, waiting for the phone call.

One of the children, God bless her, had made a decision — this was either an emergency or she had forgotten the rules. She stood on a chair with the phone in her hand, talking. Oh, children, even the flesh, in this weak light, offers no clarity.

The Way It Looked

THERE WAS A SMALL MAN STOPPING to pray on the sidewalk as they drove west toward the edge of the city. The car windows were open and they had the heat at their feet. The dirty wet streets were all covered with leaves. The man in the brown coat might not have been praying but he stood there silently, not looking around, not asking directions, and just as they drove by he looked to the sky.

In the old days some of the trees would have had fruit on them this time of year. Adam told that to his wife. He didn't know what she was thinking.

"I don't think so," she said.

"What?" he asked. He couldn't hear from the sound of the heater on their feet. She liked the cool air to breathe, but his feet got so sore from the cold. His feet cramped and curled as he aged. There would be fewer and fewer good days.

"Sorry, Judy. I didn't hear."

"I don't think so," his wife repeated. "I think the apples would be gone by now, anyway."

"Oh," he said. "When do they pick them?"

She turned to him from the window and the sudden movement of her head caught his eye, so he looked at her.

She was smiling, reaching down to take her socks off. Her feet were too hot. Her straight hair was white and short; no hint of the dark brown of her youth, or the dyed reddish black of her more recent past.

"When they're ripe," she said.

They were barely moving. She was looking at him and he pulled over to the curb to look back. It was the wrong thing to do.

"Let's just go," she said. "Let's get going."

"Hang on there, Jude. I'm sorry, but that's a long drive coming up. I've got to get out and stand a bit. I've got to walk a little. Let's just take a walk."

She stared at him, smiling a straight smile. When he was angry at her, when they had been having a fight for some reason when they were home, he hated that smile. It was smug and it hurt him. When they were in the city and met someone they knew, someone who was cruel, he liked that smile.

"I'm sorry to hear about David," someone would say on the street.

"Oh, what did you hear?" Judy would ask, smiling.

"Oh, you know. I'm just sorry for his trouble."

"That's very kind of you," Judy would say, and reach out to rub the person's arm. "He's fine. He'll be all right."

Adam loved her then, and they would continue down the sidewalk, away from the person who was asking questions but who wouldn't come right out and say it, but he knew not to speak to her.

~

During the funeral he'd held Judy's hand. He could read her through this, he thought. He could know whatever she felt. At the time he was only watching the preacher. He was never one for hymns but he loved the preacher's voice; it wasn't deeper than usual, or louder, but it was calmer; its authority came from somewhere within, as a preacher's should, but rarely did. It wasn't the words; Adam quickly stopped hearing the words.

The preacher's angular body moved correctly, like a clock — its arms with set tasks, its ability unquestioned — his long fingers hung down the sides of the dark podium, or stretched out at the ends of his reaching arms and pointed to the ceiling, or curled slightly inward to make the hands small baskets when he spread wide his arms in a shrug of supplication.

Adam sat in the middle of the right front pew, with Judy on his right and David's widow, Aspen, on his left. Almost immediately he had stopped watching the preacher's face and instead followed his hands. A man like that is used to speaking to the dying and the dead, he knew, but still, Adam was impressed by how surely his body behaved, and how strong the hands looked, even though they were just holding air.

Then, near the end of the preacher's unheard words, Aspen had taken Adam's left hand and he held it as firmly as he could. He gently squeezed Judy's hand on his other side as the preacher's body suddenly broke its pattern of symmetry and the right arm alone reached above the preacher's head. The palm was up and the fingers closed to a point then tugged down in a rough gesture that brought them all back to the words in the air.

"We cannot know when it is our time," the preacher said, letting his hand hang empty at his side.

~

Now, at the side of the road, he wanted his wife to put on her socks and come with him.

"My feet get too sore, Judy. You know that. I just want to loosen up."

"You go," she said. "I'll just wait here."

He undid his seatbelt and looked out the windshield. The day was still grey and nobody was on the street ahead of them. It must be too cold. Or was it a school day? He couldn't tell anymore. Since he'd stopped working he sometimes had to be reminded of the day of the week. The sidewalks were empty under big trees. No children, and, with the car no longer moving, no breeze.

"Let's walk back there a bit, Judy. Just a block or two, so I can loosen up. Then I won't need the heat on so high on my feet."

She reached over and rubbed his knee.

"You go," she said. "I just want to stay here."

"I saw a man back there. He was stopped all alone. I think he was praying."

"A man with a face like that, anything he did would look like praying," she said. "You can't see his eyes without thinking he's begging."

"I didn't see his face," he said.

"Or worse, that he pities you because for this one second, on this particular day, you're taking the time to look at the world around you, and just one time, just one day off, that's it. One day without praying. Today, you're not going to pray."

He could see she was crying now, though she looked out the window away from him. He knew by the way her thumb moved around inside the curled fingers of her hand. And he knew by the way their son had died and he was too young. He knew by the way they had both loved him. He knew by the way they wanted to help Aspen though she didn't like them and never had. He knew by the way his wife had been looking anywhere as they drove, anywhere that was cold and grey, anywhere there were no people.

Everything he needed to know he knew by his wife getting too hot and by him getting too cold. He knew by just believing what she said, that the old man they'd passed was the kind of man who always looked like he was praying, or begging.

He put his hand on his wife's shoulder and drew her to him. He felt her wet cheek on his neck and it was hot. She was cooking in here. Neither of them mumbled anything and when they left each other on the opposite sides of the car, Adam's eyes were crying too. He cleared his throat and said, "You're right," and put the car into drive and drove.

He knew she was right by thinking back. He knew she was right because the old man probably spent days there, with his arms open wide, waiting for something bitter to fall from the tree, something shaped like an apple, something that never does fall, but used to. Or something that never had. But the old man wears the jacket with big pockets, and waits.

Build a Small Fire

THIS IS THE THIRD FUNERAL IN the last two years. The first time, flying home in the early fall, Doug stopped to buy a black jacket on his way to the airport as the cab waited on the street. That funeral was not a surprise; he should have had his clothes already. The second funeral was virtually the same, though it was a shock, and it was the heart of summer. He stood in the sun with his black clothes on, in Saskatchewan again, glad for the ceremony, glad to have someone tell him where to go.

Beginning the drive alone back to the coast after the second funeral, he tried to see what others saw of his home. They talk about its flatness. They get lost, they say, because it's all the same. But it's not; there are changes all around. That quarter he would snowmobile on as a child is fenced now. Someone's drilling a well in the southwest. They're letting that small stand of poplar grow. He used to sit there with Lena some Sunday afternoons. They would build a small fire. They had a shelter there and nobody came looking. They weren't big drinkers so the vodka she stole at Christmas lasted forever. Nobody could see. Nobody was looking.

There had been a cow at the edge of a dugout on the right side of the highway, to its chest in water. He saw it trying to get out, slipping, stumbling, and then standing again. He drove into the yard and steered the car around the gravelled circle to stop by the door. The heat was singeing when he stepped from his car. When he knocked on the door some teenage son looked at him unimpressed. We know. We'll get it out. You're like the hundredth person who's stopped.

Then he was in Saskatoon again. He let his car run on the street. He took off his tie and waited a minute before going in. It was so much hotter there than where he lived by the ocean and it was cool in the rental car. He remembered the perfect temperature at the viewing. He'd pressed his hand on his dead nephew's chest, trying to be sure. He wanted to be cool, but a neighbour came by and knocked on his window, motioned to turn off the car but he pretended not to understand. The neighbour had quite a vocabulary but eventually went back into his house.

With the other mourners he ate a Nanaimo bar and walked around looking at all the pictures in the house. And the pictures were all over, as if it had been planned. Not just the death and the reception in this room after the service, but the life itself in its photographed stages.

But this third funeral is what makes him recall the others. The first and second passed more easily, though he was closer to both those people — one a grandmother, one a nephew — than to this third dead person, who he doesn't know at all.

He drives his parents to the viewing, because it is winter and he has rented a car again. His mother has to run back and turn on their Christmas lights before he can back out the driveway. His father, in the front passenger seat, looks next door, where their neighbour is pulling his tree down the small slope to the street. His silence is atypical, yet he holds it even when his wife returns to the car. He looks out the side window all the way to the funeral home, while Doug's mother talks loudly about the man whose funeral it is.

Doug's wife and his children are not with him, and when they arrive at the viewing, he looks around for a familiar face as a reflex, and, despite himself, reaches briefly for a hand to hold sometimes, though no one is beside him. He has no friends in the small room where they have the coffee urn and stacks of white cups.

It is his parents' pastor lying in the coffin, and he walks with his mother into the room with the coffin, ready to help her across a thick edge of a carpet, if there is one, or any obstacle. He doesn't know. It is all flat, it turns out, if you follow the plastic carpet there for the snow being tracked in and lying like a path in a garden. She does almost catch a foot on the edge where it meets the soft carpet that covers the whole room, as she steps back from the coffin.

"Easy, Mom," he says, as he steps toward her. He puts a hand on her back and holds her elbow with the other.

Her wet face looks up at him, teary.

"He was such a good man, eh Doug?"

Though he doesn't know, he says yes.

"And he looks so kind," she says, still peering up at Doug. "Just like in life."

And because Doug doesn't know how a corpse might be kind, and because his mother looks at him defenseless and open-eyed, he looks into the coffin and sees the old man. At the top of a dull long-suited slim body, the head lies above a sharp white collar and solid brown tie, and the closed eyes have the look of dreaming and momentarily Doug thinks the closed-mouth smile on the face had been planted there deliberately, post-mortem, though he cannot say so to his mother, but then he recalls having seen this man twice, after all, and yes, he did look kind.

The first time was at a Tim Horton's in Fredericton, and he wouldn't have remembered him except for the second time, when he'd seen him in the Omaha airport. He tries to remember this man now, with his dead body in the room, because of the grief all around him. It is hard, though, because of the remorse he feels recalling their first meeting, when he had worked at the doughnut store. He doesn't want to think of it. The old man had come to the counter, smiling, and moving slowly.

He'd ordered a slice of pie with his coffee.

"I'm giving myself a treat today," he said. "I did something really good today."

But Doug had looked away and never looked again at the old guy's face. He took his money and said to the hurried people behind him: "Who's next?"

He'd forgotten his rudeness that day until he'd seen him in Omaha, and it hurts him more today because he would never know what the man had done that day long ago. When years later he saw the same man, alone, in the airport in Omaha, he'd tried to imagine the man's life, tried to imagine what good he'd done. If you see a guy staring out the window at the airport, how do you describe him? If you know for sure his life stretches years back and also years ahead what is your obligation? And what if, at other times, their paths had crossed, and a man without a face, acting private in a public place, was indeed this dead preacher. Seeing a dead man three times makes you think. Maybe it was more.

Does it go on beyond the wet twinkle in his eye? Because if this is an airport it changes. And it could be any day, but it could not be anywhere. A man looking out the window to his garden would not want the same things, Doug knows, and the only reason anything registers is because of his sudden recollection of the time at the doughnut store.

Maybe, though, the man wants for nothing. This is a man alone. This is what? The postmodern man — without beginning, without end — which you see in books but do not believe in.

His eyes will narrow. He will find himself suddenly looking at empty space — the glass is transparent. The wall is glass. The place appears and is it coming or going?

It's both. It is both, if it makes no difference, and this is where his eyes get wide. What decisions did he make to get here? He must be here. Is he here? Where is here?

Doug imagined the old man his own age, doing things he has done, or seen people do. The time he saw a man throw his keys on the ground in the grass, as the man's wife told him this is over, this is it. The couple were on the lawn below their balcony. The old blind lady they'd mailed things for was on her balcony beside theirs. She leaned out.

"She can't see," the man's wife hissed.

"She heard that," he said, his anxiety public now, as if it wasn't when he threw the keys.

No, that was a different man, Doug was sure, though he hadn't seen the face. It was nothing to do with this man, who probably never had such a fight with his wife.

Doug had imagined the man in his youth, and now, recalling the memory he'd constructed watching that man stare out the window, he doesn't know if he'd been unkind. He's not sure, and he doesn't want both of the two insignificant times he'd met this man whom his family now mourned at Christmas to have been less than generous. That he'd been a stranger to Doug makes it more horrible to imagine, not less.

In Omaha, he'd imagined this: Lying in bed when they were kids, naked for the first time together, hearing the sound of her parents up the drive, hearing them home early. This is the movies, the preacher as a young man said. Don't joke around, she said.

He stood naked in her bedroom in front of the mirror and watched, for a moment, himself. With the thin string hanging from his used penis, with the flushed face and scrawny body, how could he feel so strong?

Stop it, get something on, she said.

But he kissed her. She kissed him.

Then the moment on the lawn: sure the blind woman knew all — the minor indiscretion at the office, etc. His wife's mother and her poison. His wife's reticence and the new email account she'd started after her vacation.

Oh. And now the staring out the window. Is it coming or going?

He's sure now the story is unkind. He should be more generous. The indiscretions and the new email account just don't fit. That couldn't have been him.

~

It is impossible to know what he has imagined and what is real. He remembers the old man's expression across the counter at the doughnut store, then in that cold viewing room he feels he can see his eyes, though the lids are closed.

When the old man's face is staring right at you, square, his ears bracket an expression that is completely earnest. There are small plugs of black and/or grey growing from his ears. His uncontrolled eyebrows seem dry and foreign compared to his open, dark eyes. Wet eyes, that offer, that are eager, and —

Because they are new to you, you assume they are sad, because that is how sad sad would be, if you want to know the truth. But he licks his dry lips and smiles. Hello, he says, with a rich voice that cannot lie.

So, he's not here for sadness, but you are available to it. Maybe he's only open to hope because he's a believer, a man of faith, without putting too fine a point on it.

~

Okay, suppose that were true. This man died in a cold winter while shovelling snow. It was in the Christmas season and his heart, Doug supposes, was swollen, content.

He didn't smoke. He spoke to his grandson before going out into the cold. The grandson had a new job and for the first time in his life got paid for the time he took off at Christmas. The job was nothing special. Not a never-ending stint at a research hospital, not a first-line winger on a good NHL team, not even a union job with the RM. But it was a good job and the grandson had called from the top floor suite he rented with his fiancé. Her family was all fine.

They'd had turkey that day. The father-in-law snored on the couch.

Was the dead man's piety a response to sorrow on earth? Did he believe in heaven because of his miserable lot in life? No. No.

He took pleasure in a job well done. His peers may sometimes have ridiculed him but the cold concrete exposed as he shovelled gave him as much pleasure as the souls he'd saved for his God, or for the sake of the souls themselves, however you'd like to look at it.

So you've got to look somewhere else in this man's life. That's how you've come to the idea of him staring out the window of an airport building to a field of planes moving unnaturally on their tiny wheels.

He thought of the thin ankles crossed below her green skirt. He imagined the time before his marriage when he'd lusted after his wife. Sure, he'd felt the same once they were married, but it wasn't the same. It had taken him forty-three years to allow himself to enjoy this feeling.

It's okay; she's your wife.

But she hadn't been.

Now that he allowed himself this pleasure, almost anything could remind him of the sight of those ankles crossed like the brown wet legs of a colt struggling to stand. How had they gotten so tanned? What did she do in the wild grass of the yard or the poplar forest beyond?

The thin metal legs descending from the bottom skin of the plane to hold its hard wheels, for instance, might make him remember. His own wrists one day as it rained, when his gloves were so wet he'd removed them before reaching for the hand of a long-forgotten friend met suddenly and by surprise. The pale brown trunk of a tree in a pot beside the hospital's elevator.

Well, that one, at least, makes sense; the leaves of this artificial plant were the same edible green as his wife's skirt on that troubling occasion those long days ago.

But what of those who cannot marry? He knows he's lucky. He knows he's next.

So what is he doing with no luggage and no plane ticket?

I'll leave that to you.

What were you doing on that day, when nothing had to be said, when you finally allowed yourself to see the world, to see the connections from each human standing upright on the same concrete floor out into the world, where we are each too small, then back in? When one of these flesh nodes caught your eye because his face was blank and so was the wall he stared through?

He'd like one day, without close relatives and friends in the room, to be as open as this man was, staring into the mirrored darkness as if his own loving people were there with him, even though he knew he was alone. But as Doug's red-eyed mother walks out to the car on his arm and he tries to hold his breath through the thick clouds of exhaust, he forgets his father, who he hasn't heard say a word all night.

"Go help your dad," his mother says, just before he shuts her door. So he walks back in and finds his father's coat, finds his father, too. When they get to the car his father stands staring at the world around him, and tail lights and reverse lights are all lit up around him as he stands in the fog of exhaust. Doug swings his gaze around, looking for whatever has caught his father's attention. Then he looks back and sees the door open, his father bending to smile at his mother.

"Yes," his father says, though Doug doesn't know what he answers to.

But it doesn't matter anyway. What kind of great act is so small it deserves only a slice of pie on a weekday afternoon?

We All Considered This

HE WAS JUST LIKE ANY OTHER guy walking around with his age spots. He fished weeds from the dirt in front of his bay window, or he planted them, depending on your perspective. He knelt with a canvas seed bag that seemed always full. The sun was up when he was out there and his deliberate movements seemed neither to start nor end. The bag would have weeds in it, and so would the dirt; his hand would be in the dirt, his hand would be in the bag.

In the evenings he'd sit cleaned up and smiling in the shade at the front of his empty garage. He didn't drive anymore, and he had no car. He would sit in front of the open door of his garage, with his tools and rakes and supplies on tables and shelves behind him. He'd drink beer from a glass and wipe his forehead sometimes with an old white hankie.

We saw him all the time. Then one day he wasn't there. That's typical of this world. That's how it goes. Turns out he had been charged with collusion. They picked him up. He was gone for weeks, but I assumed it was natural. I would go and peek in the front window of the house — you know, in case it came on the market soon. My daughter needed a house. This one was pretty close to mine, so I'd like that.

The truth is her whole life was a shambles. Her brother had wrecked it. Her half-brother. I don't know. I was not in on the truth in the old days. I was drunk and at war — or drunk, then at war, then drunk again. It seemed to me that my youth had been the best time of my life — successful, I mean. I'd learned how to drink and when I came back from the war I already had that talent. It was a gift after what happened over there.

I needed to get fucked up. I needed the inside to match the outside — okay, green seas, blue skies; mountains climbing up God's cold skull, dreaming whatever rock dreams when fuckers like us climb all over it, trying to kill stuff we don't even admit is alive.

The stupid part was I got her to move back to town right away. It was simple. It went like this (on the telephone):

— The house down the block's up for sale.

— Is it nice?

— Great. Great price, too.

— I don't know.

— I could help with the down payment, too.

— I don't know. You need your money.

— I got lots. I got more than I need.

— How?

— I don't know. At least I made good financial decisions when I was drunk.

— Don't joke about that, Daddy.

— It's one of my coping mechanisms, it's fine, you know, I'm okay, I —

— What step is it?

— It's complicated.

— What step is it, though?

— I don't know.

— You're not in a program?

— I don't need a program. I've been sober two years, now, Jenny. It's fine.

— Uh huh.

— I'm sober. You could move in with me first.

It wasn't really simple. I forgot about that part. She really let me have it. She came home to get me into a program. I think she wanted the, I think she needed the — I mean she needs to help people. She practically destroyed her life helping her brother Troy. Troy, who I never wanted to meet. He is my ex-wife's boy from a couple of years before we met. He's a couple of years older than Jenny.

— Let's go see him, she told me once.

— Why?

— Don't you want to see your son?

— He's your mother's son, but not mine.

— He's my brother. I'm your daughter.

— Why would he want to see me? I asked her, and this I remember. I was having a glass of milk. It was winter. I don't know what I was doing that day, but I needed milk for my stomach. We were at the kitchen table. Who knows what time of day it is in the winter? It can be dark almost anytime. It was dark then, but we were in the kitchen and Jenny wasn't cold but she brought me an old green cardigan. It had been my father's and she'd rescued it when she was a teenager. Now she was giving it back to me. I was shivering. I needed it.

— I think it would be good for him to meet you, she said.

— I don't know, I told her. I am not sure you're right about that. He's got his own father.

— Maybe, she said. But I'd like you to come with me. It would be for me.

Of course it would be. I always missed things like this, but usually when they were told to me straight I got them. She brought me the sweater because I was cold. I should do things for her without being told.

— Oh, I said. Sure. I'd like to meet him.

— You and Mom are so over each other, she said. That won't be weird.

— No, you're right. It won't be.

A lot of things seem simpler than they are. Jenny always found things simple. She always did the right thing. When she was younger she was a loner. She would stay in her room with her dolls. One Saturday I was just waking up, and I think her mother was out somewhere. I heard her talking in the living room. She was wearing her pale yellow dress with the straps like suspenders and a bright white shirt with short sleeves that puffed at the shoulders. Her pale red hair was in a neat ponytail and she stood with her hands clasped behind her back. Facing her, with their expressionless faces, sat Winnie the Pooh in a high chair, and a blank, dark-haired white doll on the coffee table.

— You both want the same thing, she told them. You both love each other, don't you?

Pooh and the doll didn't answer, but Jenny waited for them.

— Of course, she told them. Pooh, you look at it from Betty's perspective. She wants the best for you. She wants you to be happy. And Betty, it's hard for Pooh.

Everyone considered this last one in silence.

— You were never in the war, Betty.

I heard her voice continue as I walked quietly away. I didn't want her to know I was watching. I had to get to the washroom. I had to get something for my stomach.

~

Two days after Jenny arrived, a pair of boxes arrived on the doorstep. They were Troy's effects, or some of them. She wanted them put in the basement. She couldn't deal with them right now.

I don't know how sober people do it. She told me this while she was tying her shoes and then stretching. Her body was starting to bounce imperceptibly. She was getting ready for her run. If I had it to do over again, I thought, I wouldn't change a thing. She's turned out all right. She's healthy and she's caring — maybe every second generation ought to be sacrificed to some disease or corruption, just so the next one can learn by their example. I mean, it felt good to exercise. I lifted those boxes and took them to the basement. I put them in the corner where the old couch and recliner were.

Who's allowed to look in these boxes? I asked her, but she was gone. She'd watched me set the second box down, then she was up the stairs and off for her run. I should start running, I thought. The blood felt good moving around like that. I sat in the recliner and wondered who could look in there, what harm could it do for me to see the final bunch of stuff Troy had. We had talked about me adopting him, long ago, but some neighbours had him and he seemed happy. We did it just like they were puppies or kittens back then. People just farmed out the children. It was all secret until the deathbed confessions. Nobody worried much about happiness. Drinking wasn't always a bad thing. I mean, I never hit anyone, a child or my wife.

Then this letter arrived, forwarded. It was from a woman. The letter said, Dear Troy, in the old fashioned way. It said Dear Troy and then it went on like this: Where are you? It's been too long since we've talked and I'm clean now. I want to share my cleanness with you. Maybe you are clean too? The letter was three pages long, double-sided, and written in neat little lines. Tidy and clean, that's right. Clean and tidy writing, with the word clean in almost every sentence. It made me afraid. I was sober. What does clean mean? And how does it work when the paper's clean and you dirty it with your words that actually come from someone's imagined living life to me when I don't even know what the word means and who you are — how is that clean? The word meant cutting, the word meant clipped, it meant something had been excised, it meant an elision of some kind . . . does this mean I don't believe? Does this mean I can't ever . . . is sober actually better? At least it doesn't mean I'm so new I'm born in midair, I'm living in a clinic, I've got this artificial sheen, something clicked and I'm mean, I mean cleaner than I've ever been, etc.

I tried to ignore the letter but I kept looking at it every morning, when the sun came up. I used it three days to get my mind rinsed out. It was an excellent tool, as my legs shook and I drank my coffee and tried not to smoke, because of the chain of events (coffee–cigarette, cigarette–beer, beer–rum, rum–this time I'm dead and just when my daughter's back home). So I focused on the word and it didn't bother me as much as it first had.

Then, on the third day, a postcard slid in with my stack of junk mail. It fell out from the middle as I put the stack of flyers on the table. It was from the same woman. This one said: I hope you got my letter. I am alone now. I'm happy alone. I hope you're alone too. I think we can make it together, if we're both good alone. I'm alone. It's not lonely. And this one was signed love Alice, so she had a name. The clean letter had no name, the clean letter went on forever and Alice was so clean her name wasn't there. Now she's alone and happy, signing her name for him.

~

— Daddy, he says he's not even selling his house.

— Who?

— Roy Mortenson?

— Roy?

— He says call him Morty.

— I call him Roy. Nicknames are for kids.

— Whatever you call him. He says he's not even selling his house.

— You didn't tell him I thought he was dead, did you?

— You thought he was dead?

That was one day soon after she moved here, somewhere between the letter and the postcard. The second time she spoke to him, she had him over. The skin around her eyes was translucent. She'd just come from a run and brought Roy in through the front door.

— Morty, Harold. Harold, Morty. She sat him at the kitchen table. I put the postcard under the newspaper. Jenny said I'll be right back. She said it to me and to Roy.

We looked at each other across the table.

— Did Jenny tell you I thought you were dead?

— No.

— Good. I didn't know you were alive, but that's not the same thing.

— You're just as old as me, he said.

— I don't think so. I really don't. You're seventy?

— Almost. Sixty-eight.

— I'm fifty-seven.

He stared at me and thought about that. He was likely comparing us, and I was too. He had no hair left on the top and he kept the hair at the back and the sides cut real short, it was just white tiny bristles.

— Don't you ever see me out there gardening and mowing my lawn?

— Yeah. And then you were gone. All of a sudden.

— I'm not talking about that. That's unrelated. Did you see me out there moving around? Did I have any trouble?

— I guess not, I told him. You still look older than me. I have a guy who comes and mows. I don't like flowers.

— So what? What makes you think I'm so old? I enjoy a couple of beer out in the shade at night. I watch boxing.

He leaned over to me and ramped up the urgency a bit. He opened his eyes wide and pointed. Ramped up is current jargon. I keep up.

— I've got a heavy bag in my garage.

— What do you think I'll say now? I asked him.

— I'm not old, is all. Why would you think I was dead?

— Never mind, Roy. I'm sorry. You're not dead, okay?

— I know that. I know that.

He settled back into his chair and he was taking a small breather. He closed his eyes briefly. He put his hands in his lap. He interlocked his fingers, he held his hands and settled in. I heard Jenny stirring upstairs, getting ready to come down after her shower.

— Can I get you anything, Roy? I asked.

— Call me Morty, he said. Maybe a glass of water.

Roy seemed okay. Morty. He seemed okay, but I am not sure I am cut out for this helping stuff. I went to get him a glass of water. When I came back he was reading the postcard.

— That's private, I said.

— Not really. The mailman can read it.

— You're the mailman?

He just looked at me dumbly as I set the water in front of him and pulled the postcard out of his hand. I didn't want anything to do with him, then. Troy was none of his business. Nothing was any of his business. Jenny came into the room and I left. It wasn't out of character.

In the evening Jenny told me more about him, this old man across the street. There was an old law on the books. Roy and his wife had colluded to get out of their marriage. They had conspired to lie about certain difficulties when the truth is they loved each other and just wanted out. It wasn't what they wanted anymore. I knew Roy basically from when I was sober. That's two years. So I knew him as single and retired and poking around in his garden. Apparently there was more to it than that.

Now his ex-wife wanted back in the marriage and Roy didn't know why. He didn't want her back. So he and Jenny developed a scheme. The next night we went over to his garage where he sat sipping beer.

— I don't mind, Jenny said. You can rent it from me. That's okay. We'll pay you a bit at a time.

— Just cash. My whole life's off the books right now, Roy said.

— Listen Morty. How can we get it back on the books? How much money do you need?

— I don't know, he said, and I could see he was getting agitated. He didn't shake or anything. He wasn't going to lose his temper. His eyes just looked a little wider, a little wilder, and he looked away from my daughter.

— Let's just do one step at a time. Don't worry, I told her.

— It's true. He's good. He knows about money, Jenny told him.

~

— I thought I could quit this drinking if I thought it would kill me. If I thought it would give me a disease.

— Daddy you have quit.

— You never really quit, I said.

— So you have been in a program?

— No.

— You just said you could quit.

— If it might kill me I could.

— It is killing you. It could easily kill you. You've quit.

— It's not that simple and you're missing the point, I said. What I was trying to say is if love is all it is, if love would cause me to die, if love were the dangerous thing . . .

Where do the roots of my own quitting come from? How far back do they go? I know I am one to talk. I was saying something I am not supposed to say. The danger's unclear with booze. I am saying I would use a clean needle,

I would stop shooting up, if it would possibly kill me, but I would not stop love. I mean that even knowing about AIDS I could not stop love.

The day we met Troy at Tim Horton's went terribly for me. I was a wreck, but I was steady. I had had some drinks in the morning. I had some tomato juice. I told Jenny I was all right. Jenny's mother seemed as if she was all right too.

— Yes, Harold, she said. It's good to see you too.

I couldn't keep my end of the conversation up then. I don't know how people do it sober. I couldn't do it even with the edge off. I kept looking at her neck, which had that pebbly leather look that old skin gets. I kept remembering the smell of her skin when she and I were together. I would hold her neck sometimes when we made love. My fingertips would move along its tightest line, from the hollow where her neck met her chest, to the point of her chin when she stretched. I got lost in a fog of nostalgia. I was afraid of virtually everything and so I hardly noticed Troy.

As a matter of fact, I only noticed when he got up to go outside and smoke. He was too skinny. His own neck was jagged and sore, with its Adam's apple sheer tenderness in the air. He left a wadded-up serviette on the table. It was white, but part of it was grey and wet. It expanded slowly, like a white reptilian heart, but that's where it ended; it didn't contract. It was like a heart, but it was not a heart.

I finished my milk. I needed a drink.

— How are you, Harold? she asked, as Jenny and Troy stood outside. Jenny didn't smoke but she couldn't leave Troy to shiver on his own. Out the window I saw how perfect she was. He had blue, whiskered cheeks, silver and pockmarked, but hers were pink and clear. She looked muscled and sleek just by smiling. He shivered and his smile looked like a desperate gesture, weak and furtive.

Mary asked me again.

— How are you, Howard? And her pity was clear. Are you drinking? she asked.

— You know me, I told her. How can you ask that?

— Jenny is great, she said.

— She really is, I agreed. But I don't know if this is such a great idea.

— What?

— Telling her about Troy.

— She's not stupid. She'd find out.

— She's got too much to worry about, I said.

— Like you, you mean? There is a question mark there out of courtesy. It wasn't a question, it was an accusation, but I suppose she had the right. I'm sure she had the right.

It went like that from there. Pretty soon I didn't answer any questions. Pretty soon I had nothing to add and we sat there with her trying her best and me just waiting. Jenny and Troy had gone down the street. He was smoking a filtered cigarette when they got back. I was sure it had been a hand-rolled earlier.

She went and bought him cigarettes. I'm sure of it. She gave, you see, right from the beginning.

I took my little silver flask from my pocket and drank from it right there in the Tim Horton's.

— You said you weren't drinking, she said.

— I'm falling off the wagon just now, I told her. First one in eight years, three months, and seven days.

She pinched her lips together and tossed me a tract, a small pamphlet. It was not a charitable, Christian gesture, mind you. It said fuck you, I'm through. The funny part was she was through years before. We both were. Pretending we weren't for the sake of this tiny meeting in a doughnut store made no sense.

I put the flask away as Jenny walked in. I popped in a gum and smiled.

Jenny smiled the whole drive home.

— I thought it went well, she said. I think you and Mom get along well. You know she's not seeing anyone?

What a surprise, I thought. I didn't say anything. I didn't say much to her when she got in one of these moods. I was cold so she had the heat on, but sometimes she'd put her window down a bit and breathe in the cold air like a gullible animal, then roll it up again.

— We had the best talk out there, Dad.

— I'm really glad, Jenny.

— I think he'll be okay.

— Yeah.

— He's off to Vancouver. He's got a girlfriend who moved there.

— Really, I asked, trying to imagine her, a sick woman with big eyes and no smile. The kind that would look right through me. The kind that would look right through the world as it passed by.

— I think she's going to some kind of art school.

— Oh, I said.

What a surprise, I thought. An artist, a dead poet soon.

— Well maybe a change will do him good, I told her.

— What do you mean?

— A change is always good, I told her. I don't know, just a cliché, I guess.

She didn't want to talk about anything that was wrong with him. Then a few months later she told me she was transferring out to her company's Burnaby branch.

~

Of course things were clear afterwards. There was a lot of fog in between. Roughly what I remember is this; that my daughter wasn't sleeping. That she was in danger of losing her job. That Troy was taking money and that she cried every time we spoke on the phone. The only thing that got her home was his death. I pretended it was me she was coming home to, but when a man's sober he sees things more clearly.

~

Once a week Morty would come by and sit in the kitchen for a while, listening to Jenny tell him stories. I'd give him an envelope. I'd put it on the table in front of him and he wouldn't look at it.

— It's your money, Morty, Jenny would say. No need to be ashamed.

— I'm not. Of course, he said, waving his hands in the air.

— Fine, just let him take it how he wants, I told her, and he glared at me. He didn't like me, though I managed his money. He didn't like to think so. He's a drunk, I heard him tell Jenny. No, she said. Don't say that. He's worked hard. He's my father.

For my part, I never forgave him for reading the postcard. I stopped reading the letters, too, after that. I'm not a hypocrite. Jenny's been a good example. I don't know how she would have done it, but I kept hoping Alice would try and track us down. I kept hoping I'd walk into the kitchen someday and see two young women holding each other, and this new Alice, clean and strong, telling my daughter it would be okay, it was not her fault.

Have At It

THE BOY WAS TALKING ABOUT A simple reordering of this world he lived in. He was asking his father's advice and, so that it might come to some good, so that he might hear it, and try to understand it, he set down his orange milkshake and stopped sucking on the straw. He put his hands on the edge of the red table between them.

His father was looking out the window of the restaurant. Rain rolled down the glass and steam rose from the window's edges near the floor. He was looking out into the parking lot, where two dogs sniffed around the fence at the edge of the property. They were looking for what? Some kind of specific scent in the urine of some beast, or some tinge of blood where some winged creature had touched, and left?

"I don't know what you're talking about," his father said.

"I mean what now?" the boy said.

"It's not that simple."

Of course not, the boy thought, and pulled his tray back toward him. His father hadn't touched his own meal yet. The standard cardboard box was open on his tray, the red and blue logos on its lid hidden because of the fries that held it down. He'd ordered some kind of fish sandwich, a fish sandwich of some kind, why? Nobody likes fish sandwiches.

The boy pulled a fry from his own pile and dipped it in ketchup.

"I'm sorry," his father said.

"Don't be sorry," the boy said. "Will you finish that? You should eat."

"You can have it."

"I have to grow," the boy said, apologizing to himself for eating the fish.

Outside, while they were walking to the car, a woman about the age his mother had been was getting out of her car. The car's windows were tinted and dark. Nobody could see in; how could they see out? This was the kind of question he used to ask his father. He cupped the cigarette in his hand, which swung down by his hip, but the lady saw it.

"How old are you?" she asked.

The boy politely declined to answer. He nodded and shrugged as he'd seen so many sad men do on TV.

"Are you this boy's father?" she asked his father.

"Excuse me, ma'am, but my parents are none of your business. I am quite precocious and I would like to see you try to stop me from smoking, or limit my transfats, say."

"It's okay," his father said, putting his hand on the boy's head. "He's eight or nine."

The woman was indignant.

Oh Jesus, the boy thought. This could be it. And for smoking, no less. Foster care was the last thing he needed.

"I was only kidding," he said. "I am not too precocious."

The father smiled at the woman.

"It's a candy cigarette," the boy said. "It's my father's cigarette, actually, if this is my father. Have at it, old man," he said, handing it to his father, who smoked it the best that he could and smiled weakly, and they tried to move on.

~

Inside the van, the air was still and warm, but they kept the windows up. It smelled of hand lotion. Before the boy's mother had died, she'd liked hand lotion. She liked keeping her hands soft. She was soft. She liked the smell and she liked being completely clean. And she was clean.

"I don't really like hand lotion," his mother had told him. "I need it. My skin will peel off."

The boy laughed because it was ridiculous. "Like a plant. Like an onion?"

"You won't laugh when you're older. Everything is different then. It all changes."

"I bet it's different now," the boy said. "Technically, it is different both times, so right now shouldn't be considered the norm."

"That's the other thing," his father said, smiling at him in the rear-view mirror. "You're the last person who should be talking about norms."

"What a thing to say to your son," his mother said, hitting him on the shoulder. "He's normal. If not . . ."

"It's okay, Mom. Who wants to be normal? There's no such thing. Perhaps your friend driving the van has forgotten that?"

"Call him your dad. You're confusing him."

His father did his best dumb-guy face in the mirror and the boy couldn't stop laughing.

~

It goes back to this: they are reordering the world. They are believing some things continue even though the mother does not. Continue. Don't forget, the boy thinks, she was your father's wife, and that's why you want to keep him somewhere in the mix too. But he stares at everything as if it were exactly the same. When they play Frisbee, he catches and looks at the blue disc as if it's a puzzle that he can't be bothered to solve. When they eat, he looks at his food as if it's a chair.

~

If he were really the kind of boy that he is when he speaks, he would know what to say to his father. He would know what to say about the time he opened the bathroom door and saw the shape of his joined parents behind the plastic shower curtain. He saw their silhouettes part and his father reach out to rinse the shampoo out, then cry as hair came off in his hands.

The boy wants to see him through the rain-glazed window of the fast food restaurant investigating the edges of the property, sniffing for excrement, sickness, and blood. He wants him to cry like a boy his age and then come back inside, or step out of the steam like he did that day, when he pulled the shower curtain aside and saw him.

"Your mother is dying," he said. "And I'm sad." Then he retreated back into the shower, where the two silhouettes embraced again.

"That's ridiculous," the boy said. "We have to do something."

His parents ignored him, so he yelled. "Have you exhausted all the possibilities?!"

They just held each other, sobbing, as if they were more afraid of him than this spectre that had just been raised.

"There are new treatments every day!" he screamed.

In response, the water continued its dirty drumming on the floor of the tub when it missed his parents' bodies.

So he lunged at their dark shapes and pounded at them with his fists. The shower curtain gave way and he fell into the tub on top of it. They stared down at him, one on each side. They were naked and his Spiderman pajamas were soaked. He looked up at their wide eyes and kicked his feet all over as fast as he could.

"You dumb fuckers! Stop the water! This is stupid."

The Expert

I SAW AN EXPERT CREATING A distraction. I didn't care what my attention was to be diverted from; I wanted to see this disturbance. She was down by the wishing fountain, on the other side of the river. Beside the fountain was an iron sculpture you will swear is a dinosaur from one angle, a scale-model pickup truck from another, but when she sat down on her little stool, it was a piano.

Where did the sound come from? Where did her fingers touch that old rusted sculpture to make such music?

She closed her eyes.

I was the only one listening. A young boy stood beside me briefly, looked at me, then left. He had the same blank face the whole time. An older woman with blue hair jogged by slowly, toward the people stretching in front of Brainsport. I smiled at her. I said isn't this wonderful? I used an exclamation point instead of a question mark, but who could hear me over the large sound of the piano?

The old lady shook her head no and kept jogging.

Okay, fine. I will listen by myself. It was hard for everyone in those days — we were all supposed to be aware. A distraction expert had just as difficult a time as the real deal, the criminal or the legislator, the mediocre artist or the lobbyist.

I didn't care. I stood and watched this magnificent creature turn this cold block of rusted iron into a child's toy piano. I beamed at her as she turned that toy piano into a real, black and white piano.

As the expert finished up, the stars stayed hidden in the clear day's sky, the birds softly wondered their own polite questions, and she stood and stepped away from the sculpture. I was on my knees in the fountain, gathering change to give her.

Out of the corner of my eye, I saw a crowd of people murmuring. Hacky-sack players; mothers with babies strapped to their bodies; salesmen with BlackBerries and invisible phones; service industry types with smudged aprons; the whole gamut. Above the crowd, city officials nailed a minor celebrity to the door of a church.

The expert walked toward me and sat on the edge of the fountain. She took her sandals off and turned to face me, lowering her feet delicately into the clear water.

"It gets harder every day," she said.

"You distracted me."

"You're in love, that's all."

I looked up at her from where I knelt in the fountain. Was it really so easy? Did her thin black hair do me in by simply hanging, bluntly cut and brushing lightly her neck where the skin of her shoulders ducked in under the white of her dress? Was it her eyes, which I swear I never looked into, afraid to get too close? But here, a stone's throw from the real action, I was sure I was brighter than that.

"Nonsense," I told her, and held both hands out to her, open and full of coins. "I think it's mostly silver."

She smiled and waved the money away, dismissing the coins, not me.

"We will dry our money here," she said. "If it's taken before we get back, well . . . it was never ours anyway."

I set them on the edge of the fountain, on the lip of concrete that jutted up in a circle to hold the water in. I stood anxiously. We were going somewhere. I didn't even notice, at the time, the crazy way she talked about money.

~

"I will tell you what I am a distraction from," she said.

"Shhh," I told her. "I don't want to know." And I put my finger to her lips.

She started again: "But you have wormed your way into my heart."

"No," I said. "Let's keep it real."

"Please. No clichés," she said, closing her eyes and pressing the back of one hand to her forehead. She swooned. At least it seemed like swooning. I don't know. It was a gesture from black-and-white movies. It was as if she loved clichés, but didn't want to.

We were facing each other in the dark room at the bottom of my building. She was tempted to faint. I was tempted to catch her and race with her slender body in my arms to the exit, to the stairwell, up twenty-five flights of stairs, and up, up to the roof of the building where all the stars were visible, and all the sky in this flat world. We could spin in each other's arms, all the colours could bleed into each other and our breath could leave us.

~

There was a knock on the door.

"Answer it," she whispered.

I let go of her and she let herself fall back onto the bed.

It was a pair of suits from the city, and they were there to see her. One had a briefcase, one had a clipboard.

"I don't know her name," I told them.

"Believe us," they said, "you don't need to. The expert in your bed is the one we're after."

"Leave us alone, please," she said from behind me.

How could I? But I did what I was told, and went to the kitchen. I had four glasses of water on a tray when I came back to the room. The city people sat across from her on the loveseat. She sat on the chair by the window and signed a paper on the clipboard, then handed it to them and smiled at me.

"Some water?" I asked, and set the tray on the coffee table in the middle of the room.

We all drank from our glasses, me standing and looking at them all in turn, they only interested in the form on the clipboard. Finally they nodded and stood. One of the city officials took an envelope from his pocket and handed it to the expert.

"Everything is changing," he said, sadly.

"We are just not sure," the other one said.

"We have to evaluate," they both said.

"It's okay," the expert told them, then stepped toward me and took my hand. "I'm not sure myself."

We walked to the door and they left without another word.

~

In this day and age you don't ask questions. It was cooler than it had been in weeks. I was still amazed at the new woman walking perfectly on my arm. I was amazed by her abilities, and by the beautiful way she rolled with the punches.

"This is a good severance package," she told me. "I'm happy."

"Me too," I told her, and she leaned on my shoulder as we walked.

As we walked down the tree-lined street she let her right hand stray, touching the fences by our sidewalk lightly, making them sound first like breath over a half-empty bottle, then like a chorus of bagpipes miles away.

I told her I couldn't believe it. I said touch everything, and she smiled and quietly turned parked cars into steel guitars, trees into bass choirs.

The poor news anchor nailed to the church door was growing weary as we walked by him. He was having trouble breathing. This was his last job too, and my beautiful expert couldn't take it anymore. We pulled the nails out and laid him at the church door. She wiped the forehead above his closed eyes with a cold cloth, and I wept as her ministrations made the sound of a wet finger on a wine glass.

Another blue-haired lady ran down the street and shook her head no.

We walked slowly home, her hands clasped around my arm. She was leaning into me. Then we were naked, there in the cool dark room. You can trust me, I said, and I waited in silence to feel her, my elegant, unemployed expert.

Acknowledgements

JackPine Press originally published "A Long Day Inside the Buildings" as a chapbook, with illustrations by Drew Kennickell.

"It Cools Down" appeared in *The New Quarterly.*

"Big Books Shut" and "Leave Her Alone" appeared in *The Fiddlehead.*

"Have At It" appeared in *The Vermillion Literary Project Magazine.*

"We Don't Celebrate That" appeared in *Prairie Fire.*

"The Expert" appeared in *stonestone.*

"How Blue" appeared in *The Danforth Review.*

"He Hasn't Been to the Bank in Weeks" appeared in *The South Dakota Review.*

"We All Considered This" appeared in *The Nashwaak Review.*

"You Didn't Have to Tell Him" appeared in *Grain.*

"Whose Origin Escaped Him" appeared in *Eleven Eleven.*

Thanks to the editors of all of the above, and to the following people whose conversation and readings have helped me with these and other stories: Alana Wilcox, Mark Anthony Jarman, Brian Bedard, Corinna Chong, Andrew Pulvermacher, Alix Hawley, Frances Greenslade, Matt Kavanagh, Colin Snowsell, Michael Kenyon, John Lent, Renee Saklikar, Al Forrie, Jackie Forrie, Lee Ann Roripaugh, and some people I must be forgetting in South Dakota, and, of course, Janeen, Finley, and Lucy.